Ménage

ALIX KATES SHULMAN

a novel

OTHER PRESS
NEW YORK

Production Editor: Yvonne E. Cárdenas
Text Designer: Cassandra J. Pappas

This book was set in 11.5 pt Requiem by Alpha Design &
Composition of Pittsfield, NH.

10 9 8 7 6 5 4 3 2 1

Library of Congress Cataloging-in-Publication Data

Shulman, Alix Kates.
    Ménage / by Alix Kates Shulman.
        p. cm.
    ISBN 978-1-59051-520-4 (trade pbk. : acid-free paper) —
ISBN 978-1-59051-521-1 (ebook)
    1. Triangles (Interpersonal relations)—Fiction.   I. Title.
    PS3569.H77M46 2012
    813'.54—dc23

                                            2011047122

For CS and SW

Thou strong seducer, Opportunity!

—JOHN DRYDEN

Ménage

1   ZOLTAN BARBU COULD NOT decide what he ought to wear to the funeral. His usual attire was black, not for mourning, even less for style, but as a symbol of his disregard for material things; therefore he would have to mark himself as a mourner some other way. But how? He wished he could honor the occasion by donning the intricately patterned blue-and-mustard foulard ascot he had bought on a lark in Paris, but he knew that today any decoration, however modest, would be too festive for the funeral of someone who had been, until recently, his mistress.

Though he relied as heavily on his image as any of the Hollywood-Americans surrounding him, unlike them Zoltan, an émigré, was usually uncertain of the effects of such decisions, sartorial or social. For his ignorance of the ways of this world he felt he was not entirely to blame. In his youth, he had written a short searing satire on the state, a book that was denounced by his government and subsequently praised in Paris and the international press, at once launching him into the world of letters as a cause célèbre and flinging him out of the world of ordinary men. Following his arrest and the suppression of his previously ignored fiction and poetry along with the infamous satire, International PEN mounted a protest on three continents. After Susan Sontag took up his cause with a long, laudatory essay in the *New York Review of Books*, his reputation was made. Upon his release from prison, he chose exile in Paris, in the tradition of such distinguished dissidents as Kundera and Kiš.

Whereas before his arrest, only a handful of readers outside his country had heard of his work, now his standing in the West rose in degree as it fell at home. On the strength of Sontag's sponsorship, several translations were commissioned, and he was invited to give guest lectures at the Sorbonne. When after several years he was summoned to Hollywood by a Polish film director who had taken a fancy to him while shooting at Versailles, he decided to seek his fortune in film.

The fortune, however, did not materialize.

At first he was wooed by New York agents and publishers who assumed that his spare novels and slim volumes of verse were, like the infamous satire, political allegories worthy of their suppression in his native land. But as the years stretched on, with no substantial new work of fiction or memoir forthcoming, the publishers and agents lost interest. As for his screenplays, one was a critical success but a box office flop; another was shown at festivals but ignored by distributors; and the others came to nothing. Since his imperfect command of English led him to write imaginative scripts of few words but much action, he blamed their failure on the directors. The fact was, at fifty, able to complete little more than a treatment here, a review or scathing letter to the editor there, he had run through the "fortune" (as he thought of it) bestowed by the Polish director, despite the frugal lifestyle instilled in him by his widowed mother as she coped with austerities imposed in the name of the People by first one, then another tyrant.

Not that his meager output harmed his reputation or even proved entirely a social handicap. His lingering aura of the enfant terrible; his loping, sonorous voice enhanced by interesting English and accent; a nationality intermittently in the news (though after such long exile he was reluctant to share his opinions about the latest tragic bloodlettings in his homeland); and a speaking style that intimated he knew something mysterious and important created around him an aura of martyrdom rather than failure. This initial advantage, combined with an ability to raise a dense wiry eyebrow high over burning, "strong-gazing" eyes capable of performing, like the legendary Picasso's, feats of charisma, all set in a face of hawklike features, suspended between a trim little beard below and black curls with boyish cowlick above, rendered Zoltan attractive to certain persons, particularly those with artistic aspirations.

On the other hand, though his reputation remained high among the literati, enabling him to live by his wits, those who were unmoved by speech devoid of articles, deep stares, and glowering silences dismissed him as a sham. And given that charm must be exercised in public, whereas a serious writer must sequester himself for weeks and months in his study, his life often felt tainted by duplicity. Periodically he struggled to withdraw from the world, styling himself a monk; yet despite the need to write, he kept finding himself unexpectedly embroiled in complicated affairs of the heart or flesh that only further compromised his ability to work. It seemed to him that he spent half his time trying to avoid the contacts and commitments he made in the other half. And when he did manage to resist his pursuers long enough to return to his most promising manuscript, a story inspired by his own persecution and exile, there were pencils to sharpen, papers to organize, notes and old sections scrawled on lined legal pads to reread before he could begin to set new words to paper.

Wistfully he fancied himself a loner and rebuffed the suitors and sycophants who misunderstood his needs and distracted him from his difficult and fragile work. But sometimes he would give in to their adulation at a week of rollicking evenings in their hot tubs or by yielding to the lures of an actress—thus depriving himself of the basic necessities of a man of letters: solitude, self-sufficiency, and self-respect. If he lost the struggle with himself he felt guilty; if he won he felt deprived. Even the inspiring exceptions to his rule, which he justified in the name of Experience (the raw material of art), eventually did him in. For example, the burst of inspiration that had accompanied him and the tempestuous Verena Serena to Cuernavaca, where she was shooting scenes of her latest film, abruptly dissolved into the profound depression he called "writer's block" upon his return to L.A., forcing him to put aside his manuscript. Then, sunk in regret behind the drawn shades of his attic room, overcome by the knowledge of how little of value he had accomplished in a decade, he gradually renewed his vows to pursue the only work for which he felt himself qualified, despite the lengthening time since he'd written one word he was proud of.

Earning barely enough to sustain himself, he slipped ever deeper into despondency and debt. Reading over his once famous work, he sometimes wondered how he had ever thought it up and pulled it off. Had it been pure inspiration? A matter of luck or lucky timing? Maybe Sontag's enthusiastic endorsement had been a trap, condemning him to join those outsized Americans whose creativity dried up following sudden success, like the revered Ralph Ellison, or to die in debt and obscurity, like their giant Herman Melville. Perhaps he should never have come to the States.

As he studied his Spartan wardrobe (black jeans, black T-shirts and turtlenecks, black cloak for chilly nights, and black gloves, helmet, and leather jacket for riding his motorbike), he felt that the entire world had conspired to produce his current crisis, from the latest upheavals in Eastern Europe that overnight rendered his own story passé, to the whims of his landlord's grandson for whose housing needs Zoltan was being evicted (rather than, as the landlord claimed, for erratic payment of rent), to Maja's suicide via a vengeful dose of barbiturates only two nights after she had publicly quarreled with him at a screening.

By then she had no remaining claims on him, having weeks before dramatically confirmed their breakup by removing her toothbrush and lingerie from his garret and, rumor had it, immediately becoming involved with someone else. No matter that she had tried to pull this stunt with other men. Or that part of her allure was the classic seductress's neurotic unpredictability—alternately flamboyant and withdrawn, grandiose and self-destructive, hysterical and subdued—which left a poor fellow confused as to whether her threats were serious. He suspected the true cause of the despair that prompted her latest foray to the medicine box was that looming lethal marker, her thirtieth birthday. Did she mean to succeed? He doubted it. But everyone would probably hold him culpable anyway—out of malice, out of envy, out of lust.

What to wear? He finally settled on a shirt of hand-woven black cotton that he'd bought during the escapade in Cuernavaca. Unlike the designer shirt of palest silk that Maja had given him for his fiftieth birthday, which could be judged ghoulish to wear today, this one lacked all connection to the deceased.

2 THE FUNERAL WAS STUDDED with the sort of minor celebrities that Maja Stern, assistant to a hot casting director, had worked to collect: higher than starlets, lower than stars, with an artistic, intellectual cast. Allerton ("Mack") McKay, newly arrived from the East Coast, felt shy among them. Shy, intimidated, appalled by Maja's death, yet strangely elated too—nothing like a funeral to make you feel alive. In his pinstriped suit carefully tailored to flatter his short, thick body, he strained to hear the rundown of notables a man was delivering to the attentive woman in a scanty yellow sundress who sat beside Mack: Andrew Ram, two-time Emmy winner; Chip Foster, former director of the Cambridge Rep; the video artist Jasmine; a famous composer of computerized sci-fi scores who had once been Maja's lover; a girl band huddled near the back with three British rockers in shiny lavender shirts—evidently black was no longer de rigueur for funerals here. Mack recognized the names as some of the very ones Maja had managed to drop artfully into their conversations, like plump prize shrimp in a bouillabaisse.

He was impressed. Even though he alone would have been dining tonight with Maja at La Mer had she not chosen instead to dine alone on Seconol, he still had to keep reminding himself that he had as much right to be here as anyone. An unmitigated success in his own world, he lacked credentials in this one. Just that month the company that bore his name had earned him a coveted membership in the exclusive Young Presidents Club, whose card he carried proudly in his pocket alongside his credit cards, his pilot's license, and his Phi Beta Kappa key. His health was excellent, his hair, though beginning to gray at the temples, profuse. Short and lively as a Boston bull, compact in energy as an Idaho potato, he boasted a beautiful brainy wife who was two inches taller than he barefoot and had borne him two children. His shoes were handmade to the measurements of his unusually shaped feet (which Heather, his wife, suggested harbored sixth toes under the skin, like their cat's); despite his atypical feet and small stature, his squash game was such that younger men were often unable to beat him.

Still, as sad music gave way to silence and a long-thighed blonde clicked up to the podium to launch the personal testimonials, Mack felt out of place and squat.

Now that his dinner with Maja was off, he wished his wife were here. Whenever he felt out of place, Heather's presence could boost his confidence. She was as lovely as any of these Hollywood types and probably a lot smarter. With her savvy eye she would get this scene in a moment and clue him in.

He turned off his cell phone and scanned the room. A striking man of strange demeanor, dressed in New York black from head to foot, stood motionless against the wall like some large predatory bird, an osprey, perhaps, or some mutant species, all bone and beak, perched to fly off if you startled him. He had a fixed scowl on his cadaverous face and the same arresting eyes reproduced on the jacket of a book Mack had intended to return to Maja that night, after carrying it around in his briefcase for more than a month without having found time to read it: Zoltan Barbu, one of Maja's lovers. The love of her life, she once extravagantly claimed—but then she had said the same thing about Mack's friend Terry, back when she was with him. Zoltan seemed the more likely candidate. They had met, Maja explained dramatically, "practically in the womb" of her mother, a poet who had been part of the same group of student dissidents as Zoltan. Though he had been arrested when Maja was seven and had fled the country soon after his release, throughout Maja's childhood her parents had praised Zoltan Barbu as a hero. The writer's stricken appearance supported Maja's claim: his cheeks were creased, his eyes feverish, his mouth drawn, and though he was not sniffling like some of the women, his lean, slightly stooped body gave an overall appearance so morose and haggard that by the time the recessional music began Mack decided to say something consoling to him if he could catch him on the way out.

3　THE CHILDREN WERE ASLEEP, and Heather was curled up with Tina the cat in the big green chair, reading a book. For her, reading was more than a pastime, like watching a movie; it was an elevating, intimate act. She read slowly, carefully, pencil in hand, marking the margins in a private code, lingering over certain passages, copying into a special notebook those words or phrases that touched her or that she thought she might like to use in her own writing, occasionally posting over her desk brief passages that spoke directly to her. Such physical acts of communion made the authors' words seem almost her own. Ideas were real to her, a well-turned phrase sparkling like a gemstone made her laugh out loud, and certain images could cloud her eyes with tears. Sometimes she was so swept up by a book that she wanted to read on to the end in a single sitting, one long caress, at the same time longing to go slowly, in order to postpone the climax, make it last. She liked to study the author's photo on the jacket, convinced of some mysterious mutual recognition.

She prized her books, of which she now owned several thousand volumes, inordinately, she wouldn't deny it. Realizing that the very survival of books—tangible, odorous, dog-eared, tear-stained, food-smeared, marginalia-enhanced, physical objects whose pages bore traces of each individual reading—was doomed under the onslaught of electronic readers, like precious species deprived of habitat, she steadfastly refused to buy a "device" (ugly word!) and speed the slaughter. On the contrary, she withdrew into her books like an addict nursing a habit. She sometimes joked that it was when their New York apartment didn't have room for another book that she finally let Mack convince her to leave the city.

But tonight she was reading fitfully. Not because that particular volume—a biography of Katherine Mansfield, rival of Virginia Woolf, passionate disciple of Gurdjieff—failed to interest her; biographies, particularly of literary women, interested her immensely. But because her husband didn't answer his phone—which probably meant he was with a woman.

She marked her place with a finger and gazed through the dark window into the invisible woods beyond. She should have known this would happen. It was a cliché, for god's sake! Give a man enough power, lock his wife away with the kids, and he will stray. If not by seeking out other women on his own, then by succumbing to their seductions. The way he flaunted his success and went out of his way to be *nice* insured there'd be women available to him wherever he went. It was not inconceivable that he was one of those men who fooled around online, maybe had a whole Internet harem.

When Tina rubbed against her leg, Heather inserted a bookmark, put down her book, and opened the sliding glass door to let her out. All at once a range of autumn smells assaulted her, and the long low hoot of an owl ("their" owl, as they considered it) lent a melody to the lush cacophony of insect, frog, and mystery sounds that penetrated from the dark forest beyond.

She stepped outside onto the deck and took deep satisfying breaths. If Mack hadn't turned into your classic restless traveling man once the children were born, she might have treasured the chance to write in this sensuous paradise and the opportunity, increasingly rare for women since the advent of the two-earner family, to care for her children herself—at least until they were both in school full-time. But with his rapid elevation to what was plainly becoming the big time, Mack was not a man to resist the usual power perks, even at the price of undermining their harmony. It angered her that he would risk so much for so little—or what she hoped was so little; and it annoyed her that she felt so threatened by an unknown other that she could no longer muster the concentration required to lose herself in a book.

There was still enough residual light for her to see the profile of mountains, standing against the sky like sentries.

Not that Mack flaunted his affairs or was indiscreet; he was so discreet that she had virtually nothing to confront him with. Still, there were too many signs to ignore: his guilty gifts to her; his evasive behavior when he returned from a trip; the way he disappeared in his plane every Sunday of the increasingly rare weekends when he was home; and most tellingly, her inability to reach him, though he knew it made her anxious when he turned off his phone. Her various hypotheses had narrowed down to one: Maja Stern, Terry's ex, according to Mack a notorious seducer, whose name came up too oddly and too often to be innocent. Mack's jabbering on about her whenever he returned from L.A. was a giveaway that he was sleeping with her—though it could also be viewed as evidence that he was not. Well, if not Maja, then someone else.

She did not know what to do about it. She should probably have gone back to work after Chloe was born, instead of giving in to Mack's pressure to move to the mansion he built for her (picking up two architectural awards in passing) and having another child. She couldn't disagree with Mack that hiring someone to replace her full-time at home while she became another commuter slogging through the major traffic arteries was wasteful and absurd, particularly at the price of missing the chance to watch her children develop. But the alternative was becoming increasingly clear: as Mack's power expanded, hers decreased. Given his nature, she should have vetoed the move, dream house or no. Unfortunately, his nature wasn't revealed to her until it was too late.

The owl hooted again. This time Heather responded. On they went exchanging hoots back and forth for a few exhilarating moments before the owl fell silent or flew away. But not even the thrill of engaging in call-and-response with a wild bird, as she had learned to do at summer camp, could dispel Heather's ambivalence. She wasn't sorry to be done with the frantic deadlines and the steady jockeying for position at the architectural journal where she had been an assistant editor. But she did miss the office camaraderie and the mild glory of writing a monthly column on the Ecology of Everyday Life, which at least sported her byline and made her feel useful.

Mack had promised her greater usefulness to come, dangling before her ever more seductive concessions to her green ideals. He offered to rescue a pristine mountaintop from rumored development as an industrial park by a rival consortium. He embraced Heather's alternative energy schemes, designing their house as a model of efficiency, with every appliance but the restaurant stove run by solar energy, and every usable drop of household waste recyclable. The sun would keep their motors turning, heat their rooms and water, light up their nights, and after serving all their own needs provide enough extra energy to sell as a backup source to the nearby village. Surely, he argued, she would find it worth leaving the city in order to make her vision real.

Her vision was one thing, her ambition another. It was the opportunity to indulge her ambition and test her talent for writing stirring stories that finally convinced her to move. A room of one's own and five hundred pounds a year (adjusted for inflation) was a rare privilege, one that other women at her stage of life could only fantasize about. But she also knew it was a gamble with her future. That her stories had been admired by her professors and published in college journals was no guarantee of success in the world. What if her ambition outstripped her talent and she failed to produce anything worthwhile? Then she would have sacrificed what she'd had for a mere fantasy, however alluring, and wind up with a life as limited as those her generation of women believed they had escaped. If she eventually returned to the world of publishing, she'd be years behind those who had not dropped out to have children, and if the widely reported research was correct, she would never catch up. If she didn't return, then for all her classy education she might wind up living like the mothers and grandmothers so pitied or scorned by their ambitious, successful progeny.

After she and Mack left New York, the excitement of their collaboration did seem to fulfill Mack's predictions. Working on the house with him, Heather was no less engaged than she'd been on the magazine, happier in the country than she'd thought possible. But once their "project" was completed, the rooms furnished, the kinks straightened out, their second child born, the architectural awards reaped, and Mack had moved on to other, bigger projects, Heather gradually began to feel bereft. The leisure and beauty she inhabited, for which civility dictated that she be grateful, sometimes, paradoxically, left her feeling like someone under house arrest, however magnificent the house.

The owl returned. They spoke again. Heather slipped inside and grabbed the night vision binoculars Mack had given her, then perched on the deck railing and aimed them toward a certain tall oak tree where a week ago at dusk she had briefly seen her interlocutor. No luck this time, not even with the night vision promised by the infrared illuminator could she find him (or her).

Absorbed by the demands of house and family, she had been surprised to find that with Mack away two weeks out of every three, and no one else to talk to, she had become increasingly (without pronouncing the shameful word) lonely. Françoise, who helped with the children, though interestingly European, was barely eighteen, hardly out of childhood. Carmela, the thrice-weekly cleaner, was embarrassed to speak English. Heather would rather sew up her lips than upset her mother in Topeka by revealing her discontent, nor could she confide in her sister, with whom she'd once been close but who had grown distant after Heather had moved away. As for her best friend from work, Barbara Rabin, Heather suspected that Barbara disapproved of her stay-at-home life or perhaps simply envied Heather's freedom. Whatever caused the tension, Heather feared that if she confessed her rage at Mack and her fears for her marriage, Barbara would become smug or, worse, defensive about her own. Heather's few single friends were either innocents about marriage or opposed to it; why should she confirm their preconceptions?

Perhaps if she'd been able to write her stories she would not have resented Mack's absences. But with her children at home, and even during the brief morning hours that they were in preschool, she found herself unable to summon the necessary concentration or will to work. Later, she promised herself, when she had larger blocks of time.

After a few more exchanges the owl went silent again. Heather drew another deep draft of nature into her lungs and returned to the house. When the real estate market collapsed under an avalanche of foreclosures and frozen credit, she thought it would slow Mack down, forcing him to spend more time at home. But somehow the economic catastrophe had an opposite effect. As Mack explained it to her, projects on which he'd reaped profits before the crash gave him sufficient capital to enable him to buy up newly distressed properties at a small percentage of their original market value. While his undercapitalized and overextended rivals retreated into bankruptcy, he found himself staring into the opportunity of a lifetime. Far from diminishing, his ambitions soared. He had only to hold on until the market rebounded to become a wealthy man. Meanwhile, every day presented him with new bargains to investigate or acquire.

Heather's own ambitions, which had gone underground but hardly vanished when they moved, also received a vitalizing jolt. Just about the time Jamie was finally in morning preschool, a former colleague, who had launched a new general-interest online journal, invited her to write a column on ecology. Although it did nothing to bring Mack home, and it was biweekly and barely paid, it did reconnect her to the world, if only the virtual one. With an editor awaiting her words, her discipline returned, and after that, for the few hours when the children were either at school or out in the garden speaking French with Françoise, she holed up in her study, a small, windowed room overlooking the woods, which she found the most charming and peaceful in the house. There, in her brief mornings, she researched and wrote her columns and put on hold the amazing stories she hoped to write once both children were in school full-time.

4   "ZOLTAN BARBU?" SAID MACK, skipping the formality of introductions.

Zoltan took a reflexive step backward to stave off possible intrusive intimacy before giving a clipped tentative nod.

"If it's any comfort to you," said Mack, "the last couple of times I was with Maja she couldn't stop talking about you."

Zoltan studied the stranger's face before asking, "And you are . . . ?"

"Allerton McKay, a friend of Maja's." He handed Zoltan an engraved business card.

Zoltan did not look at it but instead gripped Mack's eyes with his. "What did she say?"

"She said you have too much integrity for Hollywood, maybe even for her." Mack let the flattery take effect before pressing his conclusion: "So if she didn't blame you, why should you blame yourself?"

Zoltan relaxed a bit. "Good try, thank you, but I'm afraid her opinion no longer counts. Besides, my profession requires that I understand all persons' predicaments. Evidently, I did not understand Maja's. I dismissed her threats as manipulative . . . Your connection to her?"

Now that Maja was in no position to contradict him, Mack was tempted to use the traditional male prerogative of claiming the sexual victory that had so far eluded him but that he'd hoped to perhaps secure that very night. On the other hand, there was undoubtedly a certain moral benefit attached to proclaiming fidelity to one's wife. He didn't know which response was more likely to win Zoltan's admiration and confidence. Which was more appropriate to the circumstances? Mack whipped out his handkerchief and coughed into it for the full thirty seconds it took to weigh the pros and cons of each response before saying, "Just friends."

Unconvinced, Zoltan folded his arms and raised a skeptical eyebrow at Mack, who thus reaped the benefit of both answers.

"I knew her through Terry Josephs," Mack said reassuringly. "We were roommates at college. I used to see the two of them whenever I came to L.A. on business. I suppose you know she tried to kill herself before, after Terry told her he was moving to Australia. Luckily, she failed. So before he left, Terry asked me to stay in touch with her. In fact, I was supposed to have dinner with her tonight. Made the date a week ago. But when I called earlier today to confirm, someone answered her phone and told me the terrible news." He shook his head. "I couldn't believe it. I had meetings scheduled for the rest of the day. But I canceled them all and drove straight here."

"Everyone has a story: 'Where I was when I heard.' You only had dinner with her? That's all?"

"That's it. I'm married, and Terry's my friend." Mack was pleased that Zoltan thought Maja might have been sleeping with him when in fact, despite her ceaseless flirtation, which was as much a part of her style as her low-cut dresses, she treated him more like a girlfriend than a possible boyfriend, confiding the story of her life after a single glass of wine. Part of a generation whose artistic aspiration was to make films rather than poems, she knew early on that to pursue her dream she would have to emigrate. She worked in kitchens and mastered English in order to hurry to Hollywood. Arriving at twenty-two, she began climbing the ladder from production assistant to assistant producer until she landed a plum job in casting—less glamorous, perhaps, but more powerful. Hungry starlets befriended her and ambitious men pursued her; but her own desires, she confessed to Mack, tended toward oddball artistes and Indie filmmakers. When she met Zoltan she felt an instant bond. That he belonged to her parents' generation only enhanced his appeal.

Mack wondered: Could he have had her? Though he had the money for her, he probably lacked the panache. And if he had succeeded, without her other men to discuss, what would they have found to talk about? Unlike his usual women—the flight attendants and receptionists for whom his money was attraction enough, or the cyber dates with whom he shared some naughty pictures and sexual kicks—Maja had other intentions.

Zoltan studied Mack's card. "What exactly are Allerton Enterprises?"

"Commercial properties mainly, some mixed use, some public buildings, the occasional fantasy home. Mostly back east, but now I'm looking into a couple of interesting projects here. One's a biggie. If I can pull it off—let's just say I have high hopes for it."

"You own, you design, or you just build them?"

"Depends on the financing."

"I see. Isn't that difficult now?"

"You're right, Zoltan, shrewd observation. But in every financial crisis, there are losers and winners. This time I'm one of the lucky ones."

"How is that?"

"I've been able to acquire some exceptional properties at a fraction of their value." He couldn't help gloating.

"And you are the man she stood up tonight?" asked Zoltan, looking down at the card. "'Allerton McKay, President and CEO.'" He stared at Mack. "President? CEO?"

Mack's gaze hit the floor in affected humility and his voice dropped half an octave. "I founded the company, so I get to be prez. You want to be VP? I'll put you in business."

"Careful there, Allerton—"

"Mack."

Zoltan took a harder look. So this was the mighty Mack: Maja had said that he was loaded, but not that he was short. "Careful, Mack, I could accept. Whole new life is what I need, as far from here as possible."

A mustached man with shoulder-length, probably dyed hair and bad skin bowed before Zoltan and mumbled, "Terrible, terrible, terrible."

Zoltan lowered his great arc of a nose in a digni-
fied nod.

"We all loved her, but the pity is she didn't know
it," said the man. "Which is probably why she did
it. And now it's too late to tell her. Wouldn't she
have enjoyed this though, all this attention?"

Zoltan closed his eyes until the man was gone.

"An ex-boyfriend?" asked Mack.

Zoltan tossed back his forelock and said contemp-
tuously, "Within one week every man here will promote himself to ex-lover. What's to prevent it? See
already how they enjoy themselves at her expense?"

Mack was glad he had not claimed to be her
lover, though he could hardly deny that he too was
enjoying himself at her expense. "Not me," he reas-
serted. "As I told you, we'd only have dinner together now and then. For Terry's sake, really."

Seeing another long scrutinizing stare begin to
inhabit Zoltan's eyes, Mack said, "Let's get out of
here, get something to eat, okay? I still have my res-
ervation at La Mer."

"La Mer? I'm afraid La Mer is out of my range."

"No problem. My treat. And if you don't mind
my saying so," he confided, draping an arm around
Zoltan's back and leading him toward the exit, "you
look like you could use a decent meal."

5 AT THE FIRST RING of the phone Heather leaped up, overturning her tea. She glanced at her watch: late. Emergency? An official announcement of Mack's sudden death? She hoped that she didn't hope so, but wouldn't bet on it. She let the tea sink into the Moroccan rug, which, unlike her, seemed able to absorb everything without showing it.

His death would certainly shake things up, lift the doubt that had settled over her like mist in the valley, allowing her to see ahead to some decisive act. If he suddenly died she'd sell the house, buy a condo in the city, find a good school for the kids and enroll in the best MFA program she could get into. Or take a live-in lover and stay on here to write. If their father died in an accident, the children couldn't blame her—how often did they see him anyway?—though part of her believed there are no accidents.

She reached for the phone. Forget the insurance. Bite your tongue. Where would they be without Mack? She picked up before voicemail kicked in and heard the familiar "Hi, babe."

Only Mack, calling with lies. She moved to the floor and squatted on her haunches, back flat against the wall, and took a deep breath, marshaling her wits. "Oh, hi. Finally!"

"Believe it or not, this is the first free minute I've had all day. You weren't asleep, were you?"

"No, but you missed the kids, they've been asleep for hours." She hadn't wanted to accuse him; it just popped out. She pressed each vertebra against the wall, then slowly rose and squatted again.

"I know. But I need to talk to you, babe."

"I need to talk to you too. In fact, I've been trying and trying to reach you, but your phone was off. I tried your hotel, but you aren't there. Where are you, Mack?"

"In a restaurant. About to have dinner."

"With—?"

"Actually, a very interesting man. A writer. You've probably heard of him. Zoltan Barbu? If that's how you pronounce it."

"Yes, of course I've heard of him," snapped Heather, unable to suppress a flash of envy. She, not Mack, was the book lover. On a sudden hunch, she blurted out, "What's his connection to Maja?"

"Heather, you're psychic! Get this. Zoltan has been in a relationship with her for nearly a year now. But, uh, he's not anymore."

Was Mack boasting? Had he won Maja away from Zoltan Barbu?

"So . . . ?"

"It's a long story. I'll tell you all about it when I see you. Which is why I'm calling now. I've had to change my flight. I'll be staying here an extra day. I still have a lot of work to do. And lots to tell you when I get back."

He sounded too excited. Her stomach tightened. "Tell me now. Please." Loneliness was a weakness she could handle, but not the unpredictable demon of jealousy that lay sprawled behind her consciousness like a napping child ready to cry out at the slightest disturbance, more demanding and exhausting than a three-year-old.

"It's too complicated, babe. I'll tell you when we can sit down."

She stood up. Her mind raced ahead. He would probably try to get the house, though it was in her name. Let him buy her out—alone she couldn't afford the upkeep anyway. But if he planned to move Maja in, she'd fight him. And she'd fight him for the children too. They were hers.

By the time she hung up, Tina was whining to be let in. Heather opened the door and stood on the deck peering down the valley at the view that was supposed to make her happy, barely able to guess in the sliver of moonlight at the voluptuous colors of turning leaves stretching down one mountain and up the next. Knowing she wouldn't be able to read or sleep, she decided to go straight to her study to begin her next column.

She would write on the virtue of never having two of anything when one would suffice.

6 ZOLTAN SLOWLY SCANNED THE long menu. Gorging himself on the night of Maja's funeral was probably inappropriate; yet he found a certain poetry in being taken to dinner by one of her patrons; and how often did he get to dine at a place like La Mer? The turbot with tiny shrimp was appealing, but the restaurant was famous for its bouillabaisse. As well as the zucchini crepes. Zoltan thought vegetarian would serve his image better than fancy fish; perhaps have them as a starter.

"Sorry," said Mack, sitting down and signaling the waiter. "I always forget how much later it is back home. Ready to order?"

Zoltan knew that a man who was president and CEO of a corporation probably never had trouble choosing what to eat—much less how to work, where to live, whether or not to get up in the morning. He surely took such things for granted—unlike himself, who had quite forgotten how it felt to rise at the same time each day with a purpose and destiny. Could he even say with certainty that he was still a writer?

As the lantern-jawed waiter bent toward them, his pencil at the ready, Zoltan quickly decided on bouillabaisse, and as quickly switched to turbot.

Mack was amused to recall that the last time he had eaten at La Mer, Maja had picked at her food and self-servingly grumbled about this very Zoltan. "He complained I distracted him. So was I supposed to make myself ugly whenever he wanted to write? God, genius is impossible!" Mack thought Maja had a certain genius of her own for making even her failures sound like conquests. Not content to be exploited by the star, like an ordinary groupie, Maja had mastered the ironies of injury: "Oh, he's so charming, he can charm the birds out of the trees with one of those slingshot looks of his"—as if charm were nothing but a weapon.

Mack couldn't fathom her moods. Bubbly over the bouillabaisse, she had turned sad with the salad, spearing and dropping the same asparagus repeatedly. That troubled pout should have been a clue. Did she find him boring? He often wondered why she bothered with him. He presumed that at first she had confided in him about her conquests in hopes he'd repeat every word to Terry, her ex. (He hadn't.) Or was it just a wily way of reminding Mack that men found her irresistible? Heather once told him that attractive women used that trick to control how they were perceived. Or maybe Maja just liked to be taken to expensive restaurants. He didn't mind. Even as she sat across the table going on about other men, he was appreciating her round breasts pressing against the invariably low-cut dress, always of some arcane color, mauve or bronze or sea. He wondered if Maja spoke of him to her other friends as she spoke of them to him, and if so, what she said. He appreciated that successful men were valued in part for their buying power, and he was glad he possessed that asset. Still, he did sometimes wish that women—particularly lovely, ambitious ones like Maja—would see beyond the dollar signs. He might lack the sophistication of a Terry or a Zoltan, but he was, after all, a Phi Beta Kappa from Yale who had once, unlike most of his classmates at the Business School, had other aspirations. With his mathematical talent and his artistic turn he could have been an architect, or perhaps even a scientist—both professions that required being tuned in, as he definitely considered that he was, to the mysteries and beauties of the physical world. But he had no comparable trick to let her know it.

When the food arrived Zoltan took a moment to sniff at the fragrant steam with his distinguished nose and admire the visual artistry of the plate.

"*Bon appétit*," said Mack. They clicked glasses and sipped before tucking in.

Mack couldn't get over the coincidence that his dinner companion on the night of Maja's funeral was the author of the very book—a novel called *Fire Watch*—she had pressed on him the last time he'd seen her. A gold sticker on the jacket announced that it had been short-listed for a literary prize, and there was a strong blurb for another book from Susan Sontag. Then maybe Maja did see something more in him than his balance sheet? He had planned to read the book on the plane, but what with the amazing pink-to-magenta sunset that accompanied them east and his laptop beckoning, he never got around to it. The truth was, like everyone else, he no longer had time for books. He'd intended to return it to Maja tonight, but since Zoltan had abruptly entered his life upon Maja's exit, Mack decided to give it another try. If he still couldn't get through it, he'd present it to his wife to impress her, as Maja had perhaps used it to impress him.

Watching Zoltan greedily consume his fish as if he hadn't eaten in days, Mack wondered what would be his price. Not that he knew exactly what Zoltan offered for sale, but he did know everyone had a price. How much? And for what? Whatever Zoltan had on offer, Mack wanted a piece.

Zoltan savored each succulent bite of turbot. Whenever he ate fish in the seafood palaces of France or America, perversely he thought of the river fish he had caught as a boy to present to his mother, which had invariably been small and bony, with large, useless heads. He smacked his lips. "Excellent! First-rate. Rich people know how to live." He put down his fork and stared at Mack, head atilt. "Exactly how rich are you, McKay?"

"Rich I'm not. But I have enough for everything on this menu."

Zoltan stuck out his lower lip, awaiting a better answer.

"All right, I'll tell you. I have buildings or projects in four states and prospects in two more. Not bad for someone who founded my company less than eight years ago. I built myself a home on a mountaintop that won me some awards, and next spring I'm adding a tennis court. In that house I have a good and beautiful wife, two small children, one of each. Last month I got my pilot's license, which permits me to fly my little Piper whenever I like. Of course, no one around here knows my name, Maja wanted me only as a dinner companion, and I've never written a book. Hell, I've never even written an article. But I don't think I've done too badly, considering."

Zoltan raised one eyebrow, pursed his lips, fixed Mack with a deep and glittering stare, and slowly shook his head, producing a strange cross between a smirk and a smile, his guru look. "Considering? . . . Considering?"

"Considering I'm only thirty-six," said Mack, feeling stupid the moment it was out, given the age at which people made their fortunes nowadays. Bill Gates and Steve Jobs, Mark Zuckerberg and Biz Stone—practically babies when they earned their first million, or billion. But they weren't in real estate, he kindly reminded himself.

Zoltan colored his voice with familiarity. "Come clean, McKay. Tell me who you really are."

Mack looked puzzled.

"Your card says 'President and CEO.' Is that who you are?"

"Well, yes, partly . . ."

"Is that how you define yourself? Your real self?"

"Well, not really—no, of course not." Mack felt stripped a little barer with every word he spoke. How had he got into this?

"Then who are you, McKay? Exactly who are you?"

Mack hesitated under the piercing gaze, which seemed to penetrate straight to his soul. "I . . . I don't know what you mean."

Seeing Mack begin to squirm, Zoltan concentrated his gaze even harder. He knew that everyone wants to be seen, to be known. And to see was Zoltan's gift—enhanced by the combined techniques of prison interrogator and Hollywood guru: to keep asking questions, preferably in the subject's own words, until the subject gave himself up.

"You say President and CEO are partly you, but not entirely you."

"That's right."

"And?"

"And what?" said Mack, mustering the requisite show of belligerence for this dangerous line of questioning.

Zoltan ignored it. His voice softened. "You are afraid of something, Mack. It's on your face. What are you afraid of? Say it."

"You talking about the economy?"

"No."

What was he getting at? Mack put down his fork and leaned closer. "Then what?"

Zoltan raised an eyebrow. "You tell me."

Mack pushed back his chair and crossed his legs, no longer interested in the food. Not that he wasn't flattered to have his business card analyzed by Zoltan Barbu, but in the process his defenses were being undermined. Had they been Indian wrestling, he would be getting creamed. Yet somehow it didn't matter, as he felt himself suddenly, exhilaratingly exposed. It was those eyes. Could Zoltan see in him something that he was too close to see himself? Could he see right through him? With effort, Mack managed to marshal the pushback required to remain upright. "No. You tell me."

Like a bodhisattva, or a sniper, who has mastered the art of patience, Zoltan waited, toppling Mack's defenses with his gaze.

Mack was now incapable of waiting; he crumpled under the scrutiny. "An impostor? Is that what you think I am?"

"Thou sayest it, my friend," Zoltan replied as gently as possible, stifling the triumphant grin pressing against his lips. "Too much easy success, too soon. Right? Makes you feel like impostor, afraid to be found out."

Mack was stunned. Hearing aloud the secret thoughts that he sometimes whispered to himself shocked him into silence. How had Zoltan guessed?

Sometimes Mack claimed his success was a matter of random luck—good contacts (he was a Yale man), a calculation error that had made him low bidder on a key contract during his first year in the business, unearned honors. But could those advantages really be counted as luck? Luck was the shiny side, sham the tarnished side of the coin of success. Getting something for nothing—in fact, as much as possible for as little as possible—was the essence of the game. Risk and reward: the greater the risk the less deserving of reward. The opposite of what they taught you in school. It was the same with any gamble: in the long run you lose unless you have an in or load the dice. No matter how hardworking or conscientious he might be (and he decided he was), success like his was not deserved. That was the beauty and the ugly of real estate, maybe even of capitalism. But he tried to defend himself in his usual way: "I've just been lucky, that's all."

"Same thing," said Zoltan, as if reading his mind. "Luck, cunning, charm, fraud—everything counts. Even your pose of modesty: all part of it. Now tell me, Mack, is that who you really are? If so, you must live with it. Or give it up."

Mack blushed. "Give what up?"

"You know."

Oh, he knew. The bravado. The bluff. The pretense of being someone he wasn't. He'd once dreamed of a life in science, or of a life in art. But graduating from college deep in debt (he was the first member of his family to graduate from any university, much less Yale), Mack was not so reckless as to join his classmates to denounce the fathers—not with an uncle offering to initiate him into the mysteries of real estate. He was still in debt, of course, with mortgages and promissory notes and a sometime cash-flow problem (even Trump had his cash-flow problems). But those very debts somehow enhanced his status, enabling him to expand. Yes, he knew what Zoltan meant. The Phi Beta Kappa key in his wallet, his superb collection of opera CDs, the Hockney, the Motherwell, the Wesley, the small bronze De Kooning, even the house—none of them made up for his recurrent feeling of being an impostor, an incipient failure, a fraud. He knew it as well as Zoltan did, and if he should forget it for a moment, his wife was there to remind him. But how could he change? His life was built on it. How could he "give it up"?

"How?" he whispered. "Tell me how."

Zoltan shrugged. "My telling you will not help you. Everyone must find out himself. Anyway, you would not believe me. I could maybe show you, but . . . always people resist."

"Try me."

"But you leave tomorrow?"

"We still have the rest of tonight."

The waiter cleared away their plates and handed them dessert menus.

"Come on," urged Mack. "It's a beautiful night. I'd like to see the ocean. Whenever you want I'll take you back."

"Okay. I accept. With pleasure."

Mack let out a sigh of relief. "Good. Then it's settled. Now, what'll it be for dessert? Maja particularly liked the chocolate decadence."

Zoltan closed the menu. Having found his stride, he allowed the postponed grin of triumph to spread across his lips as he proposed, "Soufflé Grand Marnier for two."

———

HEATHER CONCLUDED HER DRAFT and closed her laptop. Why did she find it so easy to write her columns but so difficult to compose her stories? The need to save the planet was urgent, and the market for fiction fading; yet it was to art, not politics, that she aspired. Irrational, she knew. An audience for her columns was practically guaranteed, while her stories, if they were published at all, would probably find homes only in obscure literary journals, supposing there were any left to publish in by the time she was ready to submit them. Still, to her, one was a job, the other an achievement, perhaps a calling. Even if she were reduced to self-publishing, which reputedly no longer carried the stigma it had before the Internet, she was determined to try. Self-indulgent? Anachronistic? Doomed? She didn't care.

But she was getting ahead of herself. As of now, she had no stories; she had a family. She turned off the light on her desk, then walked downstairs to check on her sleeping babes. Chloe lay supine, with her hair fanned out across her pillow and her arms spread wide, like a tiny diva. Her wondrous eyelashes, dark and thick, fluttered as Heather tenderly tucked in the flannel sheet. In his room, Jamie, tush elevated and thumb resting inches from his half-open mouth, emitted periodic grunts. Were they intimations of a grown man's snore or the dream sounds of construction equipment? The moment she tried to cover him he kicked himself loose.

She tiptoed out of the room and across the hall. In her giant marital bed she brooded about what stories she would write when the time came. In college she had written one about a sophisticated girl's alienation from her loving but hopelessly clueless Midwestern family, whose only god was money, and another, called "An Embarrassment of Riches," which won the senior fiction prize. Back then, her teachers had encouraged her, but now she was on her own.

With Mack unreachable and her mind churning, she sought the soporific satisfaction of self-love— nothing compared to what Mack could have any time or place he liked, but preferable to Ambien.

7 MACK PARKED THE RENTAL car in the turnaround and walked down to the beach. Waves rolled onto the shore and out again, leaving a luminous edge of white foam. Zoltan kicked sand; Mack scooped up pebbles and tossed them back to the sea while they exchanged stories: one of ascent, the other of decline.

"I had been working badly for some time. I thought Maja would be good for me, make life stable. But she made life worse. So needy, so manipulative! Took every chance to subvert me until I could not work at all. Did you know we both come from same city, I knew her parents?"

"Yes, she told me."

"Maybe because we talked in our own language, she never stopped talking. Left me no space to think. Finally, I offered to compromise: once a week I will be hers. Whatever she wants, I will do. Go out, stay home, I sleep at her place, she comes to spend night in my humble attic—whatever she wants, as long as in morning she leaves. Weekly, regularly, and otherwise she leaves me alone to work.

"She agreed. For one week. Then she started backslipping, as if one little foot inside my door could keep it always open."

"This is so different from what she told me," said Mack. "She told me she'd been living with you but you exploited her and then kicked her out."

"Living with me! What imagination! I permitted her to leave nothing more than one toothbrush and one nightgown. But she thought that being my mistress permitted her to say anything to anyone." He scowled his face red. "One day I saw that if I wanted to work I must break with her, not even let her stay one night per week." He pulled his cloak more tightly around himself.

"I hated to do that. I had so much hope to start with. I hoped she could cure me of depression, help me write again. She said she wanted to, but she really didn't. All she really wanted was attention." He sighed. "She was movie-star beautiful, you agree?"

"Yes, Maja was a beautiful woman." Mack shook his head. "What a waste."

"Beautiful but, even more, infuriating," said Zoltan, narrowing his eyes. His words, now ornamented with accent, rose over the surf. "After I broke off with her, she still would not leave me alone, she kept calling me morning and night so I couldn't work, driving by in her red car, Mini Cooper, making scenes, dripping tears. She was the most impossible, aggressive, seductive, manipulative woman. Her suicide is a triumph of manipulation and revenge!"

Mack was surprised by Zoltan's venomous outburst at the newly dead. "The way she told it," he said, "the more she gave, the more you withheld. She thought you didn't appreciate her. But then she probably thought no one appreciated her."

"Possessive, grasping female. She wanted to possess a writer but made it impossible to write. Killing the hen with gold eggs. You know that fable?"

Mack laughed. "Of course. We say goose. Hen, goose, whatever—it's universal."

"Universal. Also ironic: in one more month our problem is solved. Because my landlord is throwing me out. In one month I will be gone from L.A., and she could tell people anything she likes.

Relationship will be—I mean *would have been*—how do you say?—moot."

Suddenly Mack whiffed an opportunity. "And what do you plan to do then?"

Zoltan was at a loss for plans. He picked up a stone and skipped it across the water.

"Let me ask another way," said Mack. "What would you like to do?"

"Get away from this city of angels who are devils in disguise. Go someplace calm where I can write. Perhaps I can find some artists' colony where I can think and work. You know there are these marvelous places in woods where writers are fed and revered?"

"Really? How do you get invited?"

"No. To give readings, to write reviews you are invited. For colonies you must apply, obtain recommendations, humble yourself. Fortunately, a kind poet at UCLA with whom I once shared a podium helped me apply to MacDowell Colony in New Hampshire, where I spent two excellent months three years ago."

Excellent and also useful, he might have added. At MacDowell, where most of the artists were still "emerging," Zoltan was delighted to find himself again at the apex of the literary hierarchy. Courted and adulated, he felt his confidence soar. In his cabin in the woods, where his lunch was daily delivered to his door in a picnic basket, he completed a draft of an entire chapter of his novel. Even better, a monthlong affair with the critic Rebecca Shaffer and a useful friendship with the left-wing novelist Abel Krankowitz opened doors for him: after Rebecca wrote an admiring essay that garnered him a flurry of new attention, his satire was reissued to renewed acclaim. Abel Krankowitz, who was planning to take a semester's leave to complete his own new novel, proposed that Zoltan teach his creative writing class at the New School, in New York City, and threw in his Greenwich Village studio apartment gratis. During that semester in New York, in the company of an expanding circle of literary friends, Zoltan felt almost as appreciated as he had in Paris—until the semester ended, the novelist reclaimed his apartment, and Zoltan returned to California.

"I am probably too late to apply for this year. Maybe instead I can find some quiet family with room to let. Is it perverse to believe that somewhere are people leading normal, honest lives according to old virtues—you know, kindness, mutual aid, loyalty? Instead of complicated Hollywood plots."

Above them a meteor shot across the sky, fizzled, and fell into the sea; beneath, moonlit waves hurled themselves onto the shore and immediately backed away. The world was in ceaseless motion, teeming with possibilities. For a moment Mack forgot that he had been gaining weight alarmingly and that his feet hurt him, especially the left, despite the custom orthotics in his handmade shoes. He felt the pocket where he kept his wallet with the pictures of his house and family. "Come on, let's go back to the car. I want to show you something."

"YOU LIVE HERE?" ASKED Zoltan, peering at the picture under the map light. "You built this house?"

"Yup," said Mack proudly. "Think you could get some real writing done in a place like this?"

Zoltan drew back his head and searched Mack's face in the thin yellow light. Could he trust his ears, or was his shaky English betraying him? Could this rich stranger actually be offering to rescue him? "Let me get this straight, McKay. You are inviting me to stay with you?"

"At least to consider it. As you can see, we have plenty of space. We have guest rooms galore, and if it's woods you want, we have enough woods to hide an army of guerrillas."

Where, Zoltan wondered, was the flaw? "For how long?"

"I don't know. We'll have to see if we're the family you're looking for."

"Well, my man, this is confoundedly generous of you. But, if I may ask, why do you invite me?"

"There's something you offered to show me a while ago that I'd very much like to see."

"Ahhh!" said Zoltan softly, drawing out the syllable in a knowing sigh. "You mean how to live honestly?"

"You could call it that."

Zoltan sensed that a bargain was being struck, but he couldn't make out the terms. "I'm flattered. But won't your wife have something to say about that?"

"Heather?" A glow of pride lit Mack's face as he took from his wallet a color photo of a tall, freckled young woman in a white tennis dress, head tilted, arm shading her eyes from the sun, smiling at the camera. "Well, of course I'll discuss it with Heather first, naturally she'd have to agree. But I already know what she'll say."

"Which is?"

"She'll be tickled."

"Why?"

Mack couldn't tell him that his wife was a sucker for writers and that bringing one home to her would be a major coup. Instead he slapped Zoltan on the back and pronounced with a dash of irony, "Maybe *she'd* like to know how to live, too."

They studied the picture, Mack's favorite, a reminder of the time he first saw her in the physics lab in his senior year at Yale. She looked like a pre-Raphaelite painting—bright, gauzy hair haloing her face in little waves like ripples in a lily pond. Slim and rosy, with pale freckled skin, high cheekbones, oval, green-flecked eyes set wide apart, full hips, long fingers, narrow feet. He had been unable to stop staring at her, a perfect pearl on that beach of men. That scrubbed, privileged Middle American look. (Her family had made a killing in plumbing supplies in the post–World War II boom, gaining them admission to everything Topeka society offered, including the possibility of moving out and up.) How intimidated he'd felt by her, even though she was a freshman and he a senior. That she had trusted him enough to marry him he'd counted as proof of his potential. She was still his amulet against the philistine—though a less potent one since they'd left the city.

In fact, Heather had lately grown so suspicious and restive that sometimes Mack dreaded returning home at night. And the less he went home the more resentful she grew and the less he went home. The children, born yesterday, were now in pre-school and growing older every week. Soon they'd both be gone all day. When he bought the Piper he had hoped it would restore adventure to their lives. But instead of accepting it as a magical gift, Heather refused to fly in it or even let him take the children up. She accused him of giving her presents only of things that he wanted for himself. (With the Piper she might have had a point, but surely not with the art, the jewelry, the wine, the Prius.) What would she have to say if he could deliver her Zoltan Barbu, to help along her career and maybe spice up their marriage?

"Heather's a little older now, but she's still the prettiest, smartest woman I know. I bet she's read more books than you have. In college she won prizes for her stories. Maybe if you ask her she'll show them to you."

A warning flare, like the beginning flash of a migraine, streaked through Zoltan's brain. Was this then the catch? "Oh? Your wife writes?"

"She writes a column for *EarthBell*—the online journal? Her real writing's on hold till the kids are in school all day. She says getting out the columns is all she can do. But she has plans. And talent.

You'll see. I'm hoping you'll inspire her. I'm sure you'll like her."

In his time, Zoltan had liked several of his friends' wives a little too well, though he liked to think he'd learned a few things from experience, among them the price of disloyalty. In the thin light he studied the smile on the fresh North American face. If the arrangement were to work, he'd have to win her over. Otherwise a wife could make more trouble than a husband could guess.

Mack showed him another photo. "And here are our kids, Chloe and Jamie."

But Zoltan needed to see no more. "Very tempting offer, Mack, if sincere. Soon I hope to get a book contract, but until then, if I become desperate, I may accept."

Mack recognized the look. "You don't have to be desperate. Just come."

For a moment, something made Zoltan hesitate. He didn't understand Mack's purpose. Marriage mystified him. But after another look at the spectacular house, he decided that it was not his problem.

Hearing no objection, Mack reached into his briefcase for *Fire Watch*. "One more thing, if you don't mind. I wonder if you would sign this book for me." He handed it to Zoltan.

Zoltan was deeply pleased. "You are full of surprises, Mack. Where did you get that book?"

"You can inscribe it to Heather too. To both
of us."

Zoltan took a pen from his pocket, put it to his
teeth, and thought. He had inscribed many books,
but it was never easy in English to achieve the right
tone between close and distant, hot and cool. He
turned to the title page and wrote in his upright
European script, "*For Mack and Heather, May this opportunity enrich us all.*"

But perhaps that was too blunt, too direct? He
frowned and began a new line, softening the message with "*Toward friendship.*" Then, with an extravagant flourish that rendered all letters but the first
illegible, he signed his full authorial name.

8　FROM THE MOMENT MACK carried his suitcase through the door and kissed her, Heather knew something was up. It seemed that no sooner had she managed to adjust to his absence than she had to make room for his return. Each time he flew off on a business trip she felt danger lurking, but usually when he returned he fell into bed exhausted, and she felt safe again. This time he arrived still flying.

"I'm starving!" said Mack, dropping his suitcase and handing her a shopping bag.

She took the bag warily. Mack often brought her double-edged gifts: useless electronic gadgets, equipment she would never use, delicacies she didn't know how to serve, exotic plants destined to die. And even when he bought her things she

would never have bought herself but which delighted her—Victorian jewelry, designer clothes,
and for her last birthday an energy-efficient hybrid
Toyota Prius, there was often an ulterior motive—
some expiation or bribe—and a hidden price to pay.

She peered into the bag. "Artichokes? There must
be a dozen!" Mack was incapable of moderation.

"They were picked yesterday, the biggest, fresh-
est chokes I have ever seen, so I loaded up. What
do you think, babe?"

"They are gorgeous, Mack, but my god, so
many!"

"That's okay. We can polish off a few right now."

"A few? At this hour?"

"I'm still on California time. And don't you
know artichoke prickles are aphrodisiacs, also re-
puted to cure jet lag? Come here, you."

The kiss was passionate, maybe too passionate,
as if they had not been long married or knocked all
the way to New Jersey by having children.

He slapped her bottom affectionately. "Why
don't you get the water boiling while I hang up my
suits." He started toward the stairs down to their
bedroom (he had designed the house for maximum
energy efficiency by tucking it snugly into the hillside, with bedrooms below, under a sod roof, and

living rooms above, where skylights urged the eye upward, like the trompe l'oeil ceilings of Renaissance palazzi), and promptly slipped on a Rollerblade. Tina the cat tore up the stairs and streaked out of sight.

"Shit! Chloe!" cried Mack, breaking his fall with his suitcase and miraculously recovering his balance. Smitten, his voice turned husky with tenderness. "How's Chloe? Wait till you see the tiny things I got in Chinatown for her dollhouse. And the video games I brought Jamie."

Presents: Mack's specialty. Substitutes for Mack. Once, when Mack had telephoned home from far away, Jamie had failed to recognize his own father's voice. Heather tried to force down the bitterness that returned like acid reflux, but up it came: "How nice of you, Mack, they'll have something to remember you by."

"Want to hear what I have for you?"

"Something besides artichokes?"

"Not something. Someone."

With his eyes twinkling so roguishly, he couldn't be planning to spring Maja on her. She was confused. He was always hyper when he returned from L.A. His friend Terry had introduced him to a Hollywood crowd before moving to Australia;

since then, Mack usually came back spilling stories of starlets, producers, nude parties in hot tubs, and ready to proselytize for the latest fads: solar saunas, tantric cults, body modification.

"Someone? Tell me who."

"Patience, babe—at least till I change my clothes. I've been traveling for hours. I want to put on something comfortable. Anyway, it's a surprise." He proceeded down the stairs while Heather picked up the bag of chokes and headed toward the kitchen.

DRESSED IN JEANS AND a polo shirt that revealed the beginning of a paunch, Mack rolled a sip of coffee over his tongue as if it were fine wine; satisfied, he filled two cups with his special brew (a mixture of organic espresso and French roast from Peru) and a small pitcher with half-and-half and carried them on a tray to the study.

When they were settled at the window, with Tina curled at their feet, Heather said, "Okay—the surprise."

How to begin? "This was some trip."

Heather put down her cup. "You're teasing me. Please stop stalling. It's about Maja, isn't it?"

"How do you always manage to know these things before I tell you?"

She didn't know how she knew. But if she did know how, she wouldn't tell him. He was an innocent when it came to women; Maja's confiding in him all the details of her love life was a transparent come-on that he was too naive to recognize, but it wasn't her job to wise him up. Until this moment she'd been uncertain whether Maja had already hooked him or not yet. Now, seeing him hesitate and carefully choose his words, she was convinced they were lovers.

"Brace yourself, Heather. Maja is dead."

First doubt, then relief, like that first hit of caffeine, surged through Heather, followed quickly by something ominous. He's killed her, she thought. The nervous click-click-click of his spoon against his cup was the tip-off. She imagined the two of them driving up the coast in a rental car, his losing control, a crash—. Fear gripped her. Steadying her own hand, she reached for his and softened her voice as she did for the children when they needed her. "Tell me what happened, Mack." He was her children's father, after all; they were all implicated.

He laughed with relief at her show of sympathy. "Seems she took sleeping pills, lots of them, according to the recipe in *Final Exit*. Everyone out there has a different theory why. The point is, though, at the funeral—"

"You went to the funeral?" Heather abruptly withdrew her hand. What could be more intimate than her funeral? Even dead (if she really was dead), Maja aroused her jealousy, made her feel excluded. "You didn't mention a funeral."

"I wanted to tell you in person. It was at the funeral that I met Zoltan Barbu, the writer." On the last two words Mack's voice executed a proprietary grace note, and he bowed his head respectfully.

"Right. Your dinner date. You must have been out all night. Because your phone was off and you weren't in your room."

"I turned it off for the funeral and then forgot it. Anyway, after dinner we went to the beach to talk. A most amazing conversation, Heather, I wish you'd been there, you would have loved it. I brought back one of his books for you."

"Oh, is that the surprise?"

"Not exactly. Wait. Zoltan is taking Maja's death sort of hard. He thinks her suicide was his fault, or at least that he's being blamed for it. He can't work."

"How was it his fault?"

"They'd been more or less living together until a few weeks ago, when he kicked her out."

"Living together!" Heather's wheels whirred. Then had she been wrong about Mack and Maja? Or had the two men been rivals for her, or caught up in some complicated threesome? What charms had Maja had that she could snag two such accomplished men? Now questions spilled out in rapid succession: "Why did you never mention Zoltan before? Or didn't you know about them? How did you find out? How come they broke up?"

"Whoa! Slow down. I'm going to tell you everything in due time." He took a long swig of coffee.

"Come *on*, Mack!"

"The way Zoltan tells it, he needs to be alone to write. But she wouldn't let him. He had no privacy. So he kicked her out. But when he's alone too long he gets depressed and anxious and can't write either. So now he's in a crisis. He's being evicted from his apartment, he's broke, and he's being blamed for Maja's suicide."

"Yeah? Well?"

"He thinks if he comes to the East Coast he may be able to get a book advance from a publisher. He claims what he needs in order to write is a quote normal family life unquote." Mack took back Heather's hand before breaking the news. "So I've invited him to come live with us for a while. *If* it's okay with you."

Heather was speechless. Though she might justifiably feel outrage that Mack would invite a stranger to live with them without so much as consulting her, taking her assent for granted, in fact she was already tingling with anticipation at the prospect. Count on Mack to come up with some intriguing scheme like this just when they were slipping into a rut. Such bold unpredictable gestures were typical of him, part of what had attracted her in the first place. The audacious way he'd courted her: taking her to meet his parents on their third date, whisking her off to Puerto Rico for a weekend, obtaining magic mushrooms for her birthday. No chat chat chat like everyone else: Mack acted.

"What do you think, babe? Wouldn't hurt to have a writer around for you to talk to, would it? Besides, he seems to really need us."

Talk of extravagant gifts! Who else would take such a gutsy risk to revitalize a marriage? Unless Mack was merely making another power play, or indulging his own desire to boast a private writer in residence. Either way, to be captivated by a stranger

and invite him to share your house and family—
how impulsive, how foolhardy, how Mack!

He watched her thinking with that air of self-
containment that had so entranced him when they
met. Back then, some Yale coeds cracked under
the pressure of condescending professors and male
competition, but Heather had ignored the petty
politics and kept her own counsel. When their
physics professor had humiliated her for arriving
late to class by questioning the seriousness of her
entire sex, Mack waited for her afterward in order
to apologize on behalf of his entire sex. Her expression of incredulity combined with appreciation
was not unlike the one she wore now.

"Take your time thinking it over. Zoltan has
lots of loose ends to tie up in L.A., and he can't
come till I send him a plane ticket. Meanwhile, you
might want to read this." He handed her the book.

Heather turned the volume over slowly. Mack
knew how to get her attention. On the back jacket
she saw a picture of an intense, foreign-looking man,
dark and brooding, staring straight into her eyes.
Impressive blurbs, including one by Susan Sontag,
compared his work to Orwell, Kosinski. On the
title page was an inscription to both her and Mack
that might or might not contain a cryptic message,

one she couldn't yet decipher. She blushed at the strangely stirring prospect of waking each morning to find such a person captive in her house, ready to talk to her at breakfast—a prospect that fed every romantic fantasy she had dutifully abandoned on her wedding day.

"I don't get it," she said. "What makes him think he can live with us when he couldn't live with Maja?"

"That was different. Maja was always distracting him and making impossible demands. But we won't demand anything."

Heather knew Mack was not one to give away something for nothing. The situation was loaded; she wondered if he wasn't perhaps setting her up for some devious test. Whatever he had in mind, she was up for it. "How long would he expect to stay?"

Mack shrugged. "Everything's open. We'll see how it goes. Naturally, if it doesn't work out, he leaves."

Suddenly Heather smelled something more demanding than opportunity. "The artichokes!" She leaped up and ran to the kitchen, with Mack close behind her.

Despite the burned pot and acrid smell, Heather and Mack sat at the kitchen table stripping away the blackened outer leaves and letting melted butter disguise the faint smoky taste that had penetrated clear to the hearts. As the leaves piled up on their plates they began to explore possibilities, debating what to tell the children and where to put Zoltan. Mack assumed they'd settle him downstairs in one of the guest rooms, but Heather wondered if he wouldn't be more comfortable upstairs in her study, with more privacy and the better view. That intimate hour making plans, with the children asleep and morning still hours away, reminded Heather of the times they'd once had sitting at the kitchen table in their one-bedroom Manhattan apartment on East Ninety-second Street night after night (Mack had just begun his first ambitious complex and she was still working as an editorial assistant at a self-help magazine), planning the house they would one day build. Everything they fancied Mack drew into the plans—dream kitchen for her, workshop for him, music room, playroom for the children they would have (why not?), maybe wooded acres, spa and hot tub, solar panels, and a view. Somewhere they knew it was dangerous to pluck dreams from the air and build them of lumber and glass, like the poor fairy-tale woodsmen and fishwives who stole magic and thoughtlessly wished for what they couldn't afford. But dreams seemed innocent when they were only dreams.

Though it was after two when they finally descended the stairs to bed, they celebrated their new hopes by an intense interlude—rare since the children came—of making love.

9   ON THE SUNDAY ZOLTAN was to arrive, Heather and Mack were up at dawn, like irrepressible children in the hours preceding a birthday party. Before breakfast, Mack drove down to the hangar and took his plane up for a quick turn to dissipate some of his excess excitement. The sky was cloudless, the air bright with the crisp edge of autumn. Mack felt buoyant and powerful, as he always felt in the cockpit. His plane was too light for a long journey, but he had plans to upgrade to a small jet once the L.A. deal was consummated, Heather be damned.

When he returned home a couple of hours later, he found his wife and children outdoors collecting mums, wild asters, and maple leaves to decorate the house. Breakfast was over. He poured himself a cup of coffee from the thermos, smeared cream cheese on a bagel, and sat down at the kitchen table to watch them through the window. Against the wooded backdrop with sunlight filtering through the yellow leaves, they looked like some misty painting of autumn, or of dancers romping in a garden, he thought, trying to see them through Zoltan's eyes.

Jamie walked toward the house carrying something in his small, cupped hands. Mack opened the kitchen door for him. "What you got there, James?"

"Newts."

"Let's see."

Jamie lifted one hand just enough for Mack to see two delicate red salamanders with tiny black spots nestled in his palm. Quickly Jamie snapped the cup of his hands closed.

"Whoa, pal, not so tight. You could crush them. What are you planning to do with them?

Chloe ran through the doorway. "Mommy says we can put them in the old aquarium we used to keep the fish in, with a screen on top so Tina can't get them and they can't get out. We're going to feed them flies and fish food. Would you like me to find some newts for you, Daddy?"

"Why yes, Chloe, I'd love that. Thank you, babe."

She tugged at his hand. "Come on. I'll show you how to catch them."

"Not now, though," said Mack. "We have to get ready for our houseguest. But we can go out and look as soon as we get back from the airport."

Heather emptied an armful of flowers into the big kitchen sink and turned on the water. "Mack! Please! Don't make promises you can't keep."

"Okay, maybe tomorrow then," said Mack, backing down.

"Promise, Daddy? Promise?"

"Tomorrow's Monday," Heather reminded him. "Or were you planning to come home early?" She resented being forced to intervene.

Mack sighed. The day had just started and already she was criticizing his parenting. As if he would fail to do right by his own kids. She was irrational on the subject: urging him to spend more time with them yet not allowing them up in his plane. He lifted Chloe in his arms, hugged her. "I promise it'll be as soon as I can, babe."

Heather kissed him on both cheeks. Today was not the day to bicker. "I know what," she said. "Why don't you guys go out and get some pretty pebbles for the newts. Jamie, here's a pot you can put the newts in until I bring up the aquarium. Now go on, you two."

She looked at her watch. Only four hours until he'd be here.

Seeing Heather check her watch, Mack checked his. "I have to leave for the airport pretty soon. Do you want me to lay the fire and set up the music before I go? Glenn Gould? Monk?"

"Whatever you think."

"Okay. Then when you hear us drive up you can just light a match and throw a switch. I'll take the Porsche. Would you like me to pick up anything?"

"Some of those chocolate truffles they sell at the airport?"

She was glad Mack was going by himself. She needed the time to get ready. It would be easier for her, of course, if he took at least one of the kids along with him. When they knew she wanted everything tidy, they were usually at their most rambunctious; but she and Mack had agreed that a child in the car, even a quiet one in the back seat, might be too much family for Zoltan all at once. First impressions counted for so much.

BACK WHEN THEY STILL lived in the city, Heather and Mack had sometimes hosted witty dinners on weekends for their friends, with her startling pastas and his flaming desserts, but all that ended when they moved. Their friends from the city, reluctant to go all the way to New Jersey, preferred to meet them in a restaurant in town, and the few people who did come to visit, Mack's associates, were not friends enough to be invited to dinner. But tonight Heather was happy to devote her talents to the table. In the seldom used dining room, she set the table with linen napkins, the good crystal, a lavish centerpiece of autumn leaves and flowers, and tapered candles, as if for a party. The children were excited and impressed—enough, she hoped, to be on company behavior.

When everything that could be done in advance had been done—the bar set up, the wine breathing, the heavy cream whipped and chilling in a glass bowl, the children settled down with a movie in the playroom, and the fire, music, and lights awaiting the mere flick of a match or switch—Heather went downstairs to dress.

After wasting precious minutes trying to tame her unruly hair, she tied it back with a band and walked into her closet to pick out the right clothes. But which? From the start she had imagined herself meeting Zoltan in her burgundy silk outfit with the loose pants and fitted jacket that made her feel glamorous and bold. But now, having read Zoltan's novel, she wavered. How should she present herself? How to decide, with so little to go on? The hero of Zoltan's novel was a man assaulted by successive political upheavals and all the confusions of modernity who, in a series of adventures in the mountains of an unnamed country—as forest guide, fire watch, and pilot—manages to overcome his adversaries through defiant gestures and vigorous actions. The only significant female character, the love interest, was a powerful seductress named Ursula. The image of her, buxom and maternal, with dark eyes, small waist, smooth black hair, and a musical voice, described by the author as "bewitching," left Heather, with her small breasts, wide hips, pale eyes, masses of light wavy hair, and soft voice, unsure of her powers to bewitch. On the other hand, Ursula fails to capture the hero in the end.

Heather's only previous experience with a living writer (not counting her professors or the guys at work) had occurred the summer after her freshman year. Back home in Topeka, she'd joined a tiny group of literati who had hand-set type for both issues of a new literary quarterly in the garage of the publisher/editor, a recent Princeton graduate with a small trust fund. One day while she was setting a difficult story, its author, a friend of the publisher/ editor, stopped by to make sure there were no errors in his text. A native of the town, he was something of a local celebrity because, though still in his twenties, he had already had several stories published in prestigious magazines. Because of this, she had found herself unable to speak to him, blushing like a child when he addressed her, which only compounded her embarrassment, though he was friendly enough. That encounter probably marked the beginning of her own unspoken ambition to write. From then on, she was awestruck in the presence of writers, her awe tinged with lust. She missed no opportunity to watch them promote their books on talk shows or at book signings in nearby malls, once committing the folly of submitting to a man who had roomed at college with an eventual winner of a Pulitzer Prize. (It seemed that even in the Midwest, every community of a certain size boasted, along with its legendary mass murderer, its native son or daughter who would one day head for a coast and publish.)

Finally Heather opted for an innocent look, hoping to disarm Zoltan. Before the full-length mirror she slipped on a pair of well-cut black pants that slenderized her hips and her tailored jade green blouse (a favorite), and inserted through her earlobes the intricately cut jade pendants, a gift from Mack, that he said brought out the color in her eyes.

10   ON THE MOUNTAINSIDE, THE leaves flanking the highway were already in high flame. Mack decided to give Zoltan the royal treatment by driving home the long way around the mountain, past the most ravishing stands of maples and oaks. Instead of taking the service road directly to the back entrance, past the hangar and the neighbors' property, he would let the house appear suddenly above, regal, spectacular, and serene, even though it meant they would have to carry the bags up the long stairway from the turnaround.

While Mack walked back to the trunk for the bags, Zoltan stood up, shook out his pant legs and gazed up at the wood-and-glass edifice perched majestically just below the rounded peak. He'd known from the photo that it was more than a conventional suburban house in a wooded setting, but never had he imagined a place as grand and elegant as this. The grandeur of it, and the way the roof reached toward the sky, reminded him of the cathedral where he'd been an altar boy, only modern. He whistled long and low.

Mack stood triumphant. It was for this he had taken such risks, moved his family to the country, founded his firm, gone for the MBA, struggled through Yale, and apologized through humiliating tears to his sixth-grade teacher Miss Harrington for having scaled the auditorium rafters. For this he had sought out Zoltan, courted him, won him east from California to enrich their lives. Zoltan's whistle filled his head like birdsong, raising new hopes of transformations.

As soon as Heather heard the car trunk slam she removed her smock and ran to the living room to light the fire. Mack had taught her the standard tricks of showing real estate: maximum light, soft music, multitudes of fresh flowers. In her nervousness she scorched her hand as the flames leaped from the kindling, but she ignored the pain to flick on the lights and music. Coltrane. Count on Mack to know how to impress a European. On the way back to the safety of the kitchen, she paused at the hall window to watch Mack's familiar bull-dog frame followed by a tall slim figure in a black cloak—dramatic, operatic—mount the steps from the terrace.

At the top they rested the bags. Mack watched Zoltan's eyes follow the beams of the overhang into the foyer, on into the semivaulted living room, and out the far glass wall to the sky. "Go on in," he said, holding the door. "Heather! We're home."

Zoltan stood inside the door hearing the lush sound of jazz, inhaling the rich aromas of cedar logs and roasting lamb. The view was all that Mack claimed. And was that a Hockney on the wall? A genuine Hockney? And the books! An entire wall of them, floor to ceiling, with a ladder for access to the top shelves. "You didn't say you live in a library."

"Ah yes—the books. I didn't tell you? They're Heather's."

Heather turned off the cold water tap and gently blotted her burn with a towel.

"Honey," said Mack as she entered. He pecked her proprietarily on the cheek. "Come. I want you to meet Zoltan Barbu. Zoltan—my wife Heather." Like a shaman, Mack lightly touched a hand to an elbow of each, then stood back to admire the meeting. His best work, people said, used first-rate materials in unusual combinations to create surprising new effects. Yet all functional. A room with a view for Zoltan to work in, and for his wife an author, a book in living flesh.

And for himself? For himself? To be the one to make it happen.

Zoltan, adept at entrances, bowed over Heather's hand and lightly brushed her knuckles with his lips, her arm with the glossy lock that had fallen over his right eye. As his fingers came dangerously close to her burn, Heather braced herself but did not wince or pull away.

"Where are the kids?" asked Mack.

"In the playroom. They're staying up tonight to have dinner with us. Want to get them?"

"Not yet. Let's get Zoltan settled first. Why don't you show him his room while I bring the bags."

She led Zoltan to the study, where the last rays of sunset cast a brick-gold glow on the ivory walls.

"This will be your room—if it suits you."

Zoltan stopped and slowly turned to take in the grand view, the bouquet of mums and asters on the desk, the laptop, thesaurus, dictionary. "If!" he repeated, as the clenched fist of his life seemed to open into airy opportunity.

Heather began opening drawers and doors, like a hotel porter, displaying the bureau, the closet. "This sofa converts to a bed. I hope it's long enough for you," she said, taking in his body, immediately embarrassed at her words.

"I'm sure it's perfect. Thank you."

She led him into the sparkling bathroom with its fresh towels and small bowl of floating mums. "This is your bath."

"My own?"

"Yes. Mack used to be known for his bathrooms," she tossed off amiably.

"Splendid, splendid."

"Downstairs near us there's a guest room larger than this, but you'd have to share a bathroom with the children and our cat. This room may be small but it has the better view."

At MacDowell too there were trade-offs, Zoltan recalled. One cabin was small but had a porch; another was a long walk from the main house but had a large picture window; one was drafty, another cozy, another had a flagstone fireplace. "Yes, view is splendid."

Mack puffed in, carrying all three suitcases, and set them heavily on the floor. "Well? Will it do?"

"I hardly know what to say," said Zoltan.

"Then don't say anything. Come on, babe. Let's let Zoltan wash up. He's probably exhausted from the trip."

Mack wrapped his arm around Heather's waist to guide her toward the door, but she quickly slipped out of his embrace.

"CAN I SERVE?" ASKED Chloe when Heather began ladling soup into bowls.

"Can I?" asked Jamie.

"Not the soup," whispered Heather. "It spills. Later, maybe."

For several minutes the smooth soup of white beans and cress was ingested in contented silence. "Splendid soup," said Zoltan finally, inaugurating a slow blur of table talk.

Every time Zoltan spoke, Chloe, seated beside her mother, stared at him with widened eyes. His beard, his accent, and his daring to leave chunks of bread on the table, kept her silent and rapt. "Soup okay?" whispered Heather, to remind her daughter of its existence. But no soup could begin to compete with the absorbing stranger talking to her father, and despite sporadic efforts, Chloe barely ate, failing to respond even to Jamie's rhythmic under-table kicks.

With the main course (roast lamb accompanied by fettuccine with a lemon-flavored sauce copied from a restaurant in Rome, and olive bread, to be followed by a salad of baby greens) came the main topic. Zoltan dabbed at the corners of his mouth with his napkin, European style, and began. "I will try to be as little trouble as possible. You probably won't see me till late afternoon."

"Nonsense, Zoltan, if you'll pardon me," interrupted Mack, refilling the wineglasses. "We want you to feel at home here, just like any member of the family. Consider it your house. Right, Heather? When you're ready for breakfast, you've got to go into the kitchen and have it. Or whatever. Otherwise, we'll all be tiptoeing around each other. No, we've got to act like an ordinary family; that's the only way it's going to work. There's plenty of room here so no one has to get in anyone's way. I'm gone every day by eight anyway, sometimes earlier, and the kids are up then too. So don't worry about disturbing anyone. We want it to be completely relaxed. Isn't that right, Heather?"

"I'm sure he doesn't get up at eight o'clock, Mack. Do you, Zoltan?"

"That is somewhat early."

"We'll be the ones waking him," said Heather.

"No, no. Nothing will disturb me."

Chloe watched Zoltan tear his bread into little bits, roll them into balls and pop them into his mouth, leaving a residue of crumbs on the cloth. The way he held his fork upside down in the wrong hand and pushed his food onto it with his knife, then washed it down with swallows of wine—violations for which she and Jamie would be corrected—kept her own jaw slack and her mouth empty.

Unable to attract attention by foot, Jamie decided to see how many noodles he could pile onto his fork before the candle dripped onto the tablecloth. *Ready, get set, go,* he buzzed softly to himself, and at *go* began racing.

"Jamie!" whispered his mother. "Please, honey. Finish up nicely and you can help me serve the salad."

"We've discussed the whole arrangement," continued Mack. "One more person in a house this size will hardly make any difference. Heather sees to the meals anyway, with or without you."

"That's true," said Heather with a certain pride, starting the fettuccini around again.

"Heather is a remarkable woman," said Mack.

"Yes, I can see that already," agreed Zoltan.

"I don't know how she does it all."

Self-conscious, Heather stood up. "Would anyone like more lamb? Maybe you should carve some more?"

"Not for me, thank you," said Zoltan, "though very delicious."

"You see? Didn't I tell you?" beamed Mack.

"Please, Mack. Enough!" said Heather, heading toward the kitchen. She never knew how to respond to Mack's pimpy speeches, which felt demeaning, like being complimented on your makeup, and seemed to reflect more credit on him than on her. Why this was so was not clear; she knew only that when she tried to speak to him about it, he claimed not to know what she was talking about. He would accuse her of being hypersensitive or ungrateful or difficult to please, and she would back down. Nevertheless, in the presence of others he frequently embarrassed her.

"She's just being modest," said Mack when she was gone. "But you'll see for yourself." He started to clear the table.

"I see already. I congratulate you, Mack. She is quite a number, your wife," said Zoltan, affecting to rise.

"No, sit still. We've got a system."

While Mack carried out the platter, Heather returned from the kitchen with the salad bowl in time to catch Zoltan's last remark. "Ready to help me with the salad, Jamie?" she asked brightly, pretending not to have heard.

"Why Jamie?" asked outraged Chloe. "What about me?"

"But sweetheart, you still have to eat. Finish either your meat or your noodles and I'll let you help me serve dessert, okay? Want me to help cut it up?"

Chloe shook her head. The guest, she noticed, hadn't finished his food, either. At last she began discreetly crumbing her bread on the tablecloth.

Heather dished assorted leaves onto blue-and-white china plates. "Guest first," she whispered, handing a plate to Jamie. Jamie noticed for the hundredth time the two birds hovering above a bridge in the china pattern and wondered why they never landed. With two hands he carried the plate slowly around the table. He stopped beside Zoltan and stood waiting to be relieved of his burden, but Zoltan, energetically reducing a second piece of bread to crumbs and speaking in what sounded to Jamie like a foreign tongue, failed to notice him. While he waited, Jamie studied the bearded jaw bobbing up and down, like the jaw of a steam shovel, until, transported, Jamie began to growl softly from deep in his throat, imitating a motor and after a bit adding a soft high screech of a shovel, loaded, turning on its swivel. Only after Mack silenced Jamie with a poke and scowl did Zoltan notice the plate resting on two small hands near his elbow, awaiting his attention. Finally relieved of his burden, Jamie, thrilled and terrified to have been caught for a second in the gleaming foreign eye, raced back to his mother for another, safer plate. "No running!" admonished Chloe enviously. Heather gave them each a warning look, but fortunately the men had buried themselves in talk and did not notice the small conspiracies at the lower end of the table.

THE CROSS-CONTINENTAL FLIGHT in the 747, the fast drive, the wooded heights, the splendid house, and the extraordinarily attentive McKays gave Zoltan a heroic hope, as if the degradations of his past were about to be cleansed in the clear mountain air, as if some unimagined American miracle were about to unfold under the eye of this beneficent family. What might not be possible?

While his hostess put her children to bed and his host loaded the dishwasher, Zoltan, sated and satisfied, clasped his hands behind his back and paced slowly before the books. A surprisingly interesting collection—more literary, less technical than he'd have expected, with an entire shelf of old, leather-bound editions, and no trash. He sidled up the alphabet alongside the shelves until he found himself staring at his own name on the spines of two familiar volumes nestled side by side at eye level with the likes of Beckett, Bolaño, and Blake. He pulled out a volume of Walter Benjamin, blew dust from the top, and flipped slowly through the pages. Thoroughly read, with neat but illegible scratchings in the margins. Dare he hope, then, that these people had perhaps some intimation of who he actually was? Pleasure flushed through him until the shelves of books abruptly recalled him to his duty—to work!—which, in rapid succession, increased his resolve, doubled his doubts, aggravated his anxieties and ambitions.

He was exchanging the Benjamin for one of his own books when the sound of footsteps sent him sliding into a seat in time to avoid being caught. Only to be caught several moments later examining Heather's flushed beaming face as Mack came in.

MACK SAID, "IT'S SETTLED, then? We'll keep him?"

"Sounds good to me," said Heather.

The coffee table in the living room was mussed like a bed after love. A nearly empty cigarette pack, butts of half-smoked cigarettes cold in the ashtrays, coffee slopped into saucers, tangerine peels and grape seeds, crumpled foil from chocolate truffles, assorted glasses and their rings, an almost empty brandy bottle.

Zoltan rested his elbow on the mantel of the tall Rumford fireplace like a large bird of prey perched on a low branch. "For how long?" he asked, dangling a cigarette.

"If this works out," said Mack, "then I hope you stay at least till you finish your book."

"Heather?" said Zoltan in a low murmur, catching her in the dark gleam of his eye.

From the sofa where she slouched, Heather, who had given up smoking with her first pregnancy, lit her second cigarette of the night and blew a ring. "I say he stays as long as he's this charming."

Two small flames still flickered tenuously in the grate over a mounting hill of ash. Mack had lifted himself from the sofa and bent over the neat stack of logs to select another when he caught sight of his watch. "My god! Do you people realize it's two-thirty? I don't know about you, but I have to be up before seven."

"Two-thirty!" said Heather. "I don't feel the least bit tired though, do you? The night flew!

Doesn't it feel like we just finished dinner?" Her face was flushed, her voice euphoric.

"It's Zoltan's doing," said Mack. "Kept me up till dawn in L.A. and now half the night here. Have to do something about this."

Zoltan demurred. "I'm still on California time."

Mack indulged himself in a noisy yawn. "Not that I couldn't go on talking all night, you understand, but tomorrow's Monday."

"And Carmela is off tomorrow," added Heather.

"Well, bottoms up." Mack drained the last drops of brandy from his glass and began cleaning up.

While Mack stacked dishes on a tray, Zoltan crumpled the empty cigarette pack and tossed it onto the embers, watching to see the cellophane explode in a giddy burst of yellow spark and green flame. "If I may, I wish to propose a toast."

"Oh, do," said Heather, rising out of her slouch to lift her glass.

Zoltan squared his shoulders and cleared his throat. He raised an eyebrow and lifted his glass, then immediately lowered them both. "First, I have question. It is obvious what I gain in this extraordinary situation you offer, this writer's paradise, but not clear how you benefit."

"As far as I'm concerned," said Mack, settling down again beside Heather, "I'll be happy just to see you back on your feet able to write your book. That's good enough for me."

"Most gracious benefactor," said Zoltan, with a mock bow. Then, seriously, "But why? if I may ask."

"I like your work. I think it's important."

Though he appreciated Mack's confidence, Zoltan wondered if he could possibly produce what Mack expected of him—especially now, with the publishing world a shambles and the pressures that had driven him east beginning to ease. "When you invited me to live in your house, I believe you had something else in mind? Something, shall we say, less . . . altruistic?"

"Mack says you promised to teach us—what was it?—the art of living?" said Heather archly, tucking her legs back under her. "Something essential like that?"

"Ah, yes, the art of living," said Zoltan pursing his lips in his signature smirk. "'*Mon métier et mon art, c'est vivre.*' Montaigne."

"Meaning?" snapped Mack.

"'My calling and my art is to know how to live.' But Mack will remember I told to him that is something everyone must learn himself."

Heather tilted her head and smiled coyly. "Then why *do* we need you?"

"Ask your husband. It is he who invited me here."

"Since you're here now, I'd rather ask you."

Zoltan lowered his voice to a croon and tossed it back to her. "Tell me what you desire of me, Mrs. McKay."

"Too soon to tell."

"Then say what you hope."

Her eyes shone with excitement as she returned the intense gaze the writer had locked on her. She could not remember the last time she had received such penetrating attention, or when she had felt such giddy exhilaration. She tried to think of something to say; nothing came. Then, feeling her throat begin to tighten, she asked in a small voice, "The truth?"

"If you dare," said Zoltan.

"Come on, Heather. Tell us what you want out of this," said Mack.

"Okay." She reached for her glass. "This is easy. I hope to learn whatever secrets you have to teach us. But even if I turn out to be a lousy student, at least I'll have someone interesting to talk to."

Zoltan nodded slowly, as if sealing a pact. Again he raised his glass, and again he fixed his glittering gaze on each of them in turn, bringing it to rest on Heather.

"The toast, the toast!" said Mack impatiently.

"Here is the toast: that we each find what we are looking for."

Mack lifted his empty glass to his lips and said, "Hear, hear." But Heather drank in silence, without taking her eyes from Zoltan's. After a moment he nodded to each of them, then drained his glass, and tossed it with a grand flourish into the fire, where it shattered.

Heather was astounded. To her dismay, she felt her throat close down and tears well up in her eyes. Before the betrayal of her body was complete and the tears overflowed the lids, she snatched up the fruit bowl and hurried to the kitchen, hoping no one had seen.

11   SHE STOOD OUTSIDE ZOLTAN'S door holding a breakfast tray. It was five minutes past eleven. Once again she calculated the hours: though they'd all stayed up till three the night before, Zoltan had had a full night's sleep, unlike Mack, who'd gotten up at six-thirty, or Heather herself, who'd been listening expectantly for the first flush of Zoltan's toilet since she'd helped the children dress.

But suppose she had miscalculated and he was at that very moment hard at work? Then her interruption would be a clear transgression. If he were still asleep, she had no right to wake him, even though she had picked up fresh cream and croissants in the village after dropping the children at their school. But she had to risk it. From the moment Zoltan's lips had burned into her hand and his eyes had skewered her—no, even before that, from Mack's announcement a month ago that Maja's lover might come to live with them—she'd assumed he would become her lover, too. Not Maja but she would be the apex of this beguiling triangle. Reading Zoltan's books in bed at night to prepare herself for his arrival, studying the impossibly complicated map of Eastern Europe she had clipped from the *Times* and used as a bookmark, she had imagined his face nuzzled between her breasts or thighs, seen his intense gaze twine with her own. She wondered if his chest would be covered with hair, if he reached his climax slowly or quickly, if he cried out, if his kisses were gentle or hard.

And he? Did he think of her the same way? He must. His books revealed him as a man of passion. And those voluptuous glances and provocative questions he addressed to her: what other meaning could they have? He and Mack had shared Maja; now they would share her, and by some ancient geometry of the heart, justice would be served.

She put an ear to the door to listen for cues, aware that in an hour she would have to fetch the children home, and soon after that Françoise would arrive to play with them. Silence. With her pulse pounding in her ears, she lifted her fist and knocked.

Zoltan opened his eyes. Crisp white curtains stirred at the window, sunlight streamed into the unfamiliar room. His eyes were heavy and dry with interrupted sleep, the way they felt when Maja used to spy on his dreams in the mornings, staring down at him, her head resting in one hand, until he woke. As soon as he opened an eye she would begin speaking of her dreams until he had forgotten his own. Sometimes they would make love, but the day would usually be ruined anyway; he was not a morning person. He never complained to her about her watching him, knowing she would deny it or else denounce him angrily; still, when she killed herself he felt it as a nasty rebuke. "One minute, please," he called out, reaching for the dark blue silk kimono at the foot of his bed, the gift of a Russian production assistant who'd claimed to love him.

He opened the door to see Heather holding a tray yet seeming poised to flee. Her wavy hair was pulled back in a ponytail, her long feet were bare, and a pale lilac-colored shirt open at the throat grazed her jeans at the hip.

"Come in."

"I hope you don't mind, I thought you might like your breakfast in here this morning, since it's your first day."

"Mind? I'm . . . I'm overwhelmed. Thank you."

"By the window?"

He nodded and pulled his robe tight around his hips. If this was family life—a gentle push in the morning, someone to care for you but not too much—no wonder Mack was so productive. Zoltan took his bearings: a table before a sunny window, a sofa bed (now gaping open, barely leaving a path from the door), a desk, a computer—all he could want. And a woman to see to his needs. For the first time in months he had an intimation that he might actually begin to write again—if he could keep his life simple: eat well, rise early, work regular hours, concentrate, like any ordinary American. "Do you know what time it is?"

Heather heard the question as a reproach. "A little after eleven," she confessed, stung with remorse. "I'm really sorry." The tray was suddenly as heavy as a sleeping child, rendering her incapable of budging from the doorway. "We've all been up for hours, you see," she pleaded, "so I thought—"

"No, no. I should be up. I have work to do, and I have not yet unpacked. Come in. Please."

She squeezed past the open bed to deposit the tray on the table and poured him a cup of coffee from the thermos.

"You will join me?" said Zoltan.

"But . . . I didn't bring a cup."

"Ah, but you must get one then." As she was the gracious hostess, he would be the gracious host.

In the kitchen, her sanctuary, Heather leaned against the counter and took deep breaths as she tried to assess what was happening. For weeks she had imagined every possible form for this first morning alone together, yet now that it had begun she felt totally unprepared. She must reek of desire; it was palpable; how could he not sense it? And having invited her to join him despite their tacit rule of privacy, mustn't he return the feeling? Otherwise he would simply have thanked her and closed the door. And now? It was her house; it must be up to her to get things started. She shooed Tina out the kitchen door, took a mug from the cupboard, and hurried back just in time to see him emerge from the bathroom wiping his lips with a towel, still wrapped in his dashing kimono.

He was taken aback to see her perch on the open bed and pour herself some coffee. He did not know how to respond. Should he sit beside her or remain standing? To sit at the desk would be awkward. While he considered the alternatives he stirred sugar and cream into his cup, sniffed deeply, took a sip. "Ah . . . superb."

Heather raised her coffee mug to him, forcing herself to look steadily into his eyes, as they had done the night before.

He could not interpret her paradoxical demeanor, a strange combination of shy and shameless, modest and bold. Zoltan held up his cup and smiled back at her.

Encouraged, Heather balanced her mug and inched backward on the bed until she was leaning against the sofa back. Last night she had amazed herself when Zoltan had brought her to tears; now she was even more amazed to find herself boldly acting out her desires. It was completely out of character. When it came to defending her rights or acting on principle or standing up for the children, she could be as forceful as anyone. In the few years they had lived in this town she had campaigned to protect a nearby river and organized an early reading program for local kids. But in matters of the heart she had always been shy to the point of timidity, never the one to initiate anything. If Zoltan's demeanor had left her any doubt that he shared her desires she certainly wouldn't now be stretching out on his bed, crossing her legs modestly at the ankles, as she waited for him to make a move.

From his post near the window, Zoltan watched in alarm. Was he imagining it, or was Heather making herself at home on his bed? He set himself to spreading jam slowly across half a croissant, hoping she would reconsider and leave. But when after his first bite he looked up, he saw that not only had she not moved off but she had commandeered the entire length of the bed and was now watching him intently, her body spread invitingly across the mattress. Abashed to feel his own body respond, he put down the croissant and abruptly began to pace in the tiny space remaining. A ticklish situation. She was a devilishly attractive woman, almost more attractive this morning in her bare feet and dishabille than yesterday. All the while she lay there speaking innocuous pleasantries, she was rhythmically tapping one arched lean foot against the other in a way he thought calculated to arouse him. Or was that simply the way of these Americans, these Daisy Maes and Daisy Millers? They routinely objected to being valued for their sex yet shamelessly put themselves forward. No sooner had he extricated himself from the clutches of one of them (who would stop at nothing, even suicide, to possess him) than he seemed to have walked into the web of another. Only this time he was certain he was innocent. Her own husband had brought him here; he was sure he'd done nothing to provoke this wanton overture. Why did American men allow themselves to be led around by the nose by their outrageous wives? If he was not careful, if he didn't handle the situation with extreme delicacy, neither compromising Mack's nor bruising Heather's mysterious yet tremendous egos, he would be evicted from this Eden before he'd written a single word.

She could see that, like her, he was agitated, pacing nervously like a wary cat. She'd have liked to turn the conversation to books or writing, as she'd so often imagined, or, even better, to *them*. Allude to his promise to teach her things and cure her loneliness. But she was having trouble speaking at all. Why didn't he help her? "More coffee?" she offered, moving back down the bed till she could reach the thermos on the table.

As she leaned over the table, Zoltan saw one breast fall slightly forward behind her shirt—plump, white. He pulled his sash tighter and averted his eyes. Tomorrow he must remember to close up the bed the minute he awoke. "No, thank you. This is very pleasant, but I'd really better start to work. Still have to unpack, you know."

Was he going to let the moment pass? Could he too be shy behind the boldness of his eyes? "If you'd like me to help you . . ."

"No, thank you, really. You've done more than enough already. This breakfast—"

"Meals are part of our arrangement, remember? A small price to pay in exchange for—what was it you promised us?" Her eyes crinkled mischievously. "Happiness?"

Was she mocking him—looking up at him from his bed with those green feline eyes, inviting him to violate sacred hospitality on his very first day? If he accepted she would be able to denounce him to her husband on the slightest whim and have him thrown out without notice. But if he refused her, would she not exact revenge like any woman scorned? For a moment he wondered if this might be part of some hidden scheme of Mack's, or of a private family contest with him as prize. Either way, he must get her to leave his room at once.

He walked toward the bed and reached for her hands to pull her up. Heather felt his energy flow into her through his long fingers, felt the heat emanating from his body, though they were barely touching. That body, tall and bony and angular—the very opposite of Mack's—felt almost familiar, so perfectly had she imagined it.

As she took a tiny step toward him Zoltan pulled back and searched her eyes. No guilt there, nothing but that nervous surrender, that soft, blurred, womanly limpid look. He warded off a possible embrace by pressing his lips to her hand. "But look!" he said. "You've burned yourself."

"It's nothing. See? You've already cured it."

"Mack was right about you," he said, stepping back and twirling the ends of his sash. "If I wasn't a monk—"

She looked startled as he took her hand and began leading her toward the door. "I must dress now. But thank you for . . . all of this."

"A monk? What do you mean?"

"Ah, my dear, I intend to explain you everything one day, I want you to understand me. But now," he said quietly, his hands urging her out, "I must start on this day before it is lost."

Then she had misread him! She felt a deep blush begin its long, mortifying rise up her neck to burn her cheeks. He would see.

She looked at her watch. "Me too. It's time to get the kids. Shall I take the tray—?"

He could not risk allowing her one inch back into the room. "No, no, thank you, I will take it myself, later." And without hazarding a good-bye, he closed the door.

AS SOON AS HE heard her car drive off, Zoltan walked into the hall to listen, but the only sounds were cries of nature. He carried his tray toward the kitchen, walking slowly through the rooms, both marveling at his good fortune and trying to contain his envious disdain. In the morning light the cathedral-like great room, with its skylights, immense stone fireplace, and library, circled by windows giving onto decks and gardens, was even more imposing than at night.

In the big sunny kitchen he saw two of everything: two sinks, two ovens, two microwaves, two doors on the massive refrigerator, two sets of four burners on the stove, two dishwashers (unless one was perhaps some more obscure culinary device). He set down the tray in the adjacent pantry and systematically began to peer into every drawer and cupboard. His eyes were dazzled by piles of polished silver, forests of stemware, stacks of china of every size, appliances and gadgets whose uses he could not begin to fathom. There were cases of wines and liqueurs to rival a fine restaurant's, and every imaginable spice and condiment from all the corners of the world. One cupboard contained nothing but flower vases, another was stocked with boxes of crackers of every sort, another with empty containers and jars, another with every household paper product. It was inconceivable that anyone, even the owners themselves, could keep track of it all. A few items from each of the shelves could probably furnish most needs of a modest person. Never had he imagined anything like this. And now he lived in it.

He walked down the stairs and traversed the downstairs hall peering into every room. On one side were an exercise room, storage closets, bathrooms, and two offices, each with file cabinets, bookshelves, and a sleek flat-screened computer. On the other side were the bedrooms, with views down the mountain similar to the view from "his" room. There were two children's rooms plus a large toy-filled playroom with monster TV, and two smaller rooms—perhaps for guests? At the very end, the hall opened into a large sunny space with long views in two directions which could only be the master bedroom.

He stepped inside. Here the ceiling was high and domed, with a skylight illuminating the largest bed he had ever seen, not king but emperor! He stopped to imagine the passions enacted upon it. A glass wall gave onto a private deck bordered with potted flowers in riotous bloom. Beyond the deck a modest lawn, and beyond that the forest.

Zoltan walked past the bed, unlatched the sliding door, and stepped outside. Perfume licked at his nostrils, birdsong tickled his ears, a chill breeze raised the hair on his neck. He turned his face upward toward the sun, breathing deeply, and with his eyes closed spread his arms upward like an ancient worshipper. The voluminous sleeves of his kimono fell to his shoulders, allowing the solar energy to penetrate him through his naked arms. Fate had sprung him from prison, transported him to Paris, induced Washington to grant him asylum, and was now unexpectedly extending its bounty to this font of milk and honey. He rejoiced, vowing not to squander it.

A flock of noisy sparrows (or were they wrens?) at the feeder broke his reverie, and he noticed the gray cat perched on the railing observing him with its yellow eyes. He slipped back inside and relatched the door.

Off the master bedroom he discovered two windowless rooms, one composed of large closets, the other clearly the wife's dressing room. Each of these opened onto a marble bathroom with a mirrored wall, one with a giant Jacuzzi, the other with a glassed-in shower. The sinks were onyx bowls, and the toilets, Zoltan discovered, flushed silently. But then she'd said Mack was renowned for his bathrooms.

After relieving himself, Zoltan turned to the closets, one hers, one his. Behind the sliding doors in each were enough clothes for an opera company. Each had a small, separate closet just for shoes. Behind another door on each side was a chest of drawers, with the top drawer locked—for the jewelry and cash, he surmised. Small keys, innocent as virgins, hung inside each door. Scornful of such carelessness, he fitted the keys into their locks.

Jewelry, as he'd guessed, plus the usual top-drawer clutter: obsolete credit and membership cards, assorted keys, snapshots, empty wallets, small decorative boxes of wood, metal, papier-mâché containing studs, pins, broken jewelry. The cash, along with the financial records that might reveal the value of the entire estate (about which he was suddenly immensely curious), was absent.

Probably kept in a vault or a locked file in one of the offices.

Somewhere in the house a clock chimed many notes—like music. Best to end this exploration for today. Hereafter, he would note the hour Heather left and returned and stay safely within those bounds. He locked the drawers, replaced the keys on their ornate hooks, and retraced his steps up the stairs.

A rough bronze sculpture, about eight inches tall, of a prancing human figure with legs spread out beyond the oblong wooden base, rested on a table at the top of the stairs. He picked it up. So much energy and lift in a hunk of metal! A dancer? One of De Kooning's bronze women, perhaps? He had already seen a Hockney in this house; then why not a De Kooning? The royal treasure in the capital of his country was probably worth not much more than what he'd seen here today. Such accumulation seemed patently wicked. Any working man from his country—or any frugal man anywhere, includ- ing himself—could probably live for decades on the excess alone.

The sound of a car pulling up broke his fantasy. He put the sculpture back on the table carefully and hurried to his room.

12   THAT NIGHT OVER COFFEE, after the children had been read their stories and tucked into bed, and the adults had moved from the dining to the living room, Mack asked Zoltan how the day had gone. He meant to inquire about the writing, but Zoltan responded by praising the bed, closet, and furnishings, capacious beyond his needs, and the inspiring view.

"And did you walk straight into the kitchen for your breakfast as instructed," inquired Mack, "or did you spend the day tiptoeing around?"

For an instant Heather's green eyes and Zoltan's black ones met in conspiracy. "I'm afraid I overslept, actually," answered Zoltan; to which Heather added, "Can you imagine? We're all up practically at dawn and he's still sleeping when I get back from the kids' school!"

"Now just a minute, there," protested Zoltan, "just one minute. My body is still jet-lag. Tomorrow I will wake earlier."

"Not if we keep pulling all-nighters," said Mack, yawning noisily, though it was not yet late. Short of exhaustion, sleepiness seemed to him a small price to pay for the exhilarating uplift Zoltan's presence had already, in just one day, injected into their ordinary, torpid lives. Already the house glowed brighter, the fire blazed hotter, the food melted more deliciously in the mouth as Heather, the children, and Mack himself became more alert, more animated. Watching Zoltan pour himself a brandy from the decanter on the coffee table, Mack imagined the prose flowing, the pages proliferating under his patronage. (*And to my dear friends Mack and Heather McKay, I dedicate . . .*) They would throw a party for him when the book was done, a lavish affair with a fire blazing if it was winter, outdoors with paper lanterns around the pool if it was summer, and all the literary lights of New York to admire them.

"Why don't you tell us about your book," Mack said, settling back on the sofa beside Heather as he swirled his own brandy in a shapely snifter.

Zoltan was nonplussed. Where he came from it was considered intrusive or even rude to ask a writer to describe his current work; this was true even in Paris. But in America, with its tell-all cult of openness, there was no decorum. In his first twenty-four hours here, already wife and husband had each in their own way assaulted his privacy, as if he had come to live with them for their amusement. For the entire second movement of a Mozart quartet he managed to avoid answering. But in the end he had to oblige his benefactors, who sat respectfully on the white leather sofa, hand in hand, eager to hear one of the first descriptions known to the world of the not-yet-written book.

"Is very difficult to describe," began Zoltan. "Is about . . . about . . ." He turned away to clear his throat. "About modern man in exile, story of a young man from war-torn country, still a youth, who cannot find his way until called upon to overcome impossible impediments and become a hero. Just when he is about to make heroic sacrifice, he is caught and sent into exile where he encounters many adventures. Title is *Realms of Night*. There." He leaned back and folded his arms.

"But isn't that the plot of your other novel too?" asked Mack, alarmed.

Zoltan waved the question away. "No, no, no, this is completely different." He looked sternly, witheringly at Mack. "What I have just told you is background only."

"Oh, I see," said Mack vaguely. "Go on then."

"This story is of exile and loyalty, betrayal and love."

"Ah," said Heather.

Zoltan stood up in front of the fire. "Modern hero, you see, is not like ancient hero, Achilles, Hector, Marcus Antonius, et cetera, strong, open, loyal at all costs. Ancient hero confronted other heroes openly on battlefield and fought to death. But modern hero"—he shook his head—"he cannot confront his enemy so easily, sometimes does not know his enemy, you see? Enemy of yesterday may be ally today. Enemy may be traitor or patriot, pacifist or anarchist, regicide or suicide—like hero himself! Today, nothing is clear. So what is loyalty? bravery? treachery? What is terror? Or freedom?"

In his enthusiasm Zoltan put down his glass and began to pace, while the McKays sat rapt and uncomprehending.

He continued: "Not so easy to understand. Modern hero is sometimes antihero or madman, like Invisible Man, like Underground Man, or is saint like Simone Weil, or prisoner like Nelson Mandela. He often lives in exile, alone, isolated, searching for freedom amidst his enemies. To be hero he must be free. But can he be free? Today this is most pressing question."

Zoltan had worked himself into a state of excitement that set a vein to pulsing in his neck. He took a long swig of brandy and smoothed back his hair before looking at his bewildered, expectant audience: Mack, brow furrowed, earnestly biting his lip; Heather eagerly awaiting some unknown thing. Zoltan feared he had not made himself understood at all. Finally breaking the silence, he ventured, "Well?"

"Well," said Mack, "you've outlined the theme all right. But I'm not sure I understand the story."

"Yes," agreed Heather. "You said it's about loyalty—and love?"

"All right, here is the story," said Zoltan, beginning again. "Hero (no name yet) has fled to a new country where he experiences culture shock. Soon he is befriended by a woman he meets in a bar, Felice. She works in the hotel as a maid; she is young, hot. She takes him home and feeds him."

"Ah," said Heather, wriggling back into her seat, "that's the story."

Zoltan laughed. "No, Heather. It is only beginning." He took another sip of brandy and resumed.

"Soon hero discovers his phone is tapped, he is being watched, followed, like Trotsky. He believes there are some men from his country, traitors or patriots, he doesn't know which, waiting to enlist him. Or maybe to kill him. Always there is that danger. How can he know which? He sees them watching him. Felice is afraid. She moves him to her parents' village. He finds job in restaurant, slowly learns their language. She comes often and teaches him. They are almost happy, but always he is waiting to be found out. Always ready to flee. Always exile."

Mack nodded encouragement while Zoltan took another sip.

"He makes friends with Bill, his coworker at restaurant. He tells him nothing, but finds out that Bill knows certain things about him. How? He must find out. Well, one day, never mind where, he sees Felice kissing a man. He thinks it is Bill. Betrayed! He wants revenge! But first he must know, is this just woman's ordinary sex treachery or man's political plot against him? Thinking they don't know that he has seen them together, he decides to set a trap."

Heather did not hear a word Zoltan said after the phrase "woman's ordinary sex treachery." Was

he looking at her when he said it? She was mortified anew by that morning's events, which began
repeating in her mind like a car alarm. Nervously
she started straightening the objects on the coffee
table.

"But that is enough. You are tired, no?"

"No!" said Mack. "Go on, go on. You can't stop
now."

"You sound like a woman in bed," said Zoltan,
flashing a grin at Mack and then a sly smile at
Heather. "I'm sorry, I cannot tell you more."

"Why not?" said both McKays in unison.

Zoltan watched them sitting expectantly at attention, like spaniels at their master's feet awaiting
a promised treat. "I'm afraid now is not good time."

"You mean you don't know what will happen?"
asked Mack.

"I know in general what will happen. However,
until I have written it out in words it is not easy to
talk about. What do you think, Mack, is it enough
for editors to give me some money? I was actually
hoping that when I have enough pages to present,
you will advise me how. What to ask for, you know.
I fear I am not very good at business."

"Gladly, gladly," said Mack, swelling with mag-
nanimity. "But I might be able to advise you better
if you tell us the rest. Come on."

Mack was like a bulldog with a bone, thought Zoltan. "All right. But remember this is merely for a proposal. As they say in Hollywood, a treatment."

"Of course," said Mack, settling back, while the fire burned down to ash.

"THAT'S IT," SAID ZOLTAN. "What do you think?"

For a long moment there was only silence. For once, Mack was at a loss. Zoltan's exposition, however fascinating to hear, had left him in the dark, though without a doubt in the world that it was brilliant. He walked over to Zoltan to shake his hand and lacking anything else said, "Extraordinary!"

A gratified smile dispelled the anxiety on Zoltan's face.

"Honestly, Z," said Mack, sitting down again, "I'm surprised at how well you have it all planned out, and in such detail. I always thought you folks just make it up as you go along."

"But that is precisely what I do, make up as I go along." He looked at Heather.

Heather didn't know what to say either. She was certain that Zoltan's story contained a hidden message to her, though she could not yet discern its meaning. She picked up a tangerine from the bowl and began to peel it.

"Heather is awfully quiet," said Zoltan.

Heather passed around the sectioned tangerine. Finally she said, "I'm overwhelmed. I don't know what else to say. But I'm not sure I understand the ending—is it complete?"

Leaning against the mantel Zoltan ignored the fruit to pierce Heather with his eyes. "Exactly how it will end is one thing I try not to know in advance." Then he cracked half a smile and added ironically, "This may be my first lesson for you: endings leave to chance."

Was he trying to tell her that everything was still open between them, that she hadn't misread his desire that morning after all? His secret meanings seemed easier to decipher when his eyes were locked on hers.

"For my money," said Mack, "the less one leaves to chance, the better. I'd prefer a sound investment to speculation any time. Though I'll grant you, you can never know for sure what's chancy until the venture is complete or you've gotten out. I'll bet those editors agree with me. Let me know when you've got something down on paper, Z, and we'll plan a strategy."

But Zoltan, playing eyesies with the lovely Heather, was unaware that Mack's talk of investments and speculations might in any way apply to him.

13   SO THE FIRST ABSORBING weeks went by. Zoltan cast his spell each night after dinner, when the three gathered around the hearth with their brandy or wine to improvise upon their roles in their odd ménage à trois: Mack the impresario directing Zoltan the guru playing to Heather's acolyte. Maja Stern was never mentioned.

In the evenings, with the McKays seated on the sofa side by side, the flirtation between Zoltan and Heather seemed innocent enough, despite its occasional hot eruptions like the sparks exploding in the fireplace. But in the daytime, when Mack was away, Zoltan was forced to hide behind the closed door of his sanctuary until the children, those perfect chaperones, came shouting and tumbling home. As he paced before the window waiting for words and images that wouldn't come, acutely aware that his host was waiting too, his sanctuary sometimes felt like a cage, and he an animal doomed to sicken and die if he remained inside but be shot if he tried to escape. Two equally depressing prospects: the agonies of writer's block or the dangers of adultery. The tortures he suffered with the former made the distractions of the latter more enticing—and more necessary to resist. For both, the temptress Heather was to blame.

Heather, whose solitary morning hours had so recently been tranquil working interludes in her child-ruffled days, also found it impossible to concentrate, knowing Zoltan was ensconced upstairs. The sting of his kiss remained on her hand, each double meaning rang in her ears, as she was repeatedly jolted off balance by his alternate giving and withholding, his sybaritic nights and celibate days.

It wasn't simply his distracting presence that interfered with her work. A writer of his renown creating literature overhead made her own ambitions seem foolish. Admittedly, sometimes his writing left her puzzled (which might be attributable to bad translation), but his celebrity was indisputable. His work was invariably mentioned in articles about dissident or persecuted writers living in the

States, and his name appeared on announcements of prestigious conferences. After two readings of his last novel published in English, with its intrigue and multilayered convolutions, she suspected that his accomplishment was well beyond anything she could aspire to.

At first she had been baffled, even secretly hurt, that he never, not once, inquired about her work, despite Mack's embarrassing hints. But now she wondered if his disregard was perhaps a kindness, intended to spare her the humiliation of his judgment, rather than indifference or, worse, contempt. That talented subclass of women writers whose husbands and lovers were said to have sucked them dry or patronized them into madness—the Zeldas and Plaths and Rhyses—had no bearing on her case: Zoltan, though driving her to distraction, was not her lover, and her husband actively supported her writing. Didn't Mack claim that it was for her sake he'd invited Zoltan to live with them, to be her literary mentor and companion? By now it was obvious that Zoltan had no such intentions, and she wished Mack would drop it.

How confusing the whole question had become! Earning power aside, she'd never thought her work less valuable than Mack's until Zoltan moved in.

Her columns, besides shielding her from the dubious status of a privileged stay-at-home mom, at least helped the environment, which could hardly be said of most of Mack's projects (don't even mention the Porsche or the Piper). Yet with Zoltan writing upstairs, whatever pride she'd once taken in her work quickly disappeared. If he were suddenly to read something of hers, she'd be mortified. She was grateful for his apparent ignorance of the Internet, where her columns were posted for all to see.

WHEN FRANÇOISE ANNOUNCED THAT she was returning to Belgium to help her mother care for her father, who had suddenly fallen gravely ill, Heather struggled to hide her relief. She had already decided to ease her out. Not that Zoltan had responded to Françoise's delicate beauty or was even, as far as Heather knew, aware of it. His avoidance of the children entailed avoidance of Françoise. But Heather was aware of it—and wary. Graciously she promised to pay the girl's airfare and wait a decent interval before replacing her, in case Françoise wanted to return. In fact, however, she had already decided that instead of hiring another mother's helper, she would find an appropriate all-day program for the children, preferably one that offered a segment of French conversation. As it was, Carmela's presence in the house three days a week was quite enough restriction on her freedom.

AFTER THE PRESSURE OF life with Zoltan had been building up for several weeks, Heather decided to call up her old publishing buddy Barbara Rabin, the one friend who might understand what she was going through, and invite her and her husband, Abe ("Rabin" to their friends), to meet them for dinner in the city at their favorite Mexican restaurant from back in her working days. It would be the McKays' first social outing since Zoltan's arrival and might restore some much-needed reality.

"I can't wait to see you," said Barbara. "I want to hear all about your houseguest. I'm halfway through *Fire Watch*. Wow!"

"He's just impossible!" wailed Heather, surprising herself.

"Really? How? Let me guess: he's hitting on Françoise?"

"Don't be silly. He barely ever saw her since she was always with the children. Anyway, she's gone back to Belgium."

"Smart move, Heather, what with Schwarzenegger and the rest of them."

"It wasn't my idea. Her father got sick."

"Then what's the matter?" said Barbara. "Tell me."

She hardly knew where to begin. "First of all, he keeps us up till all hours, then he sleeps his mornings away while we wind up tortured by sleep deprivation. Sometimes I think he's deliberately trying to drive me crazy."

To Barbara, who felt more than a touch of envy, Heather sounded less distressed than exhilarated. "Then why do you let him stay?" she challenged.

"He has nowhere else to go. Besides, he's exciting to have around. And lovable, in his own peculiar way."

"Will we get to meet him on Friday? Or is he going to stay home and babysit for you?"

Heather snorted. She was not about to invite him to join them, knowing he'd turn her down. Even less could she ask him to babysit. He barely acknowledged the children's existence. No, she would call one of her regular sitters—passing over the high school nymphets on her list in favor of a widow from the village.

Mack, however, oblivious to the possibility of rejection, invited Zoltan to join them on Friday, suggesting that a break from work would do him good. But after a flurry of phone calls, Zoltan told Heather that on Friday, thanks anyway, he'd be dining with friends in Soho. He asked if he could hitch a ride into the city with her and find his own way back on Sunday.

"On Sunday! You're spending the whole weekend in New York? Where will you stay?"

He instantly regretted having spoken. He was spending the weekend at the home of Rebecca Shaffer and her husband. Though they had stayed in touch ever since MacDowell, he had not seen Rebecca since moving east. He was indebted to her for the boost in his standing that came with her essay and the reissue of his first book. But he certainly did not have to explain himself to Heather, who would probably burn with jealousy. His left eyebrow shot up. "I'm not sure you're permitted to ask me that."

His reprimand was in jest, delivered in his usual flirtatious style; all the same, Heather felt rebuffed. Sometimes he spoke to her as an intimate, inviting every confidence, but the next moment he could assume an icy hauteur, treating her like an inferior. Was that what he'd done to Maja? In absentia Maja was rapidly gaining Heather's sympathy. Between

Zoltan's volatility and Mack's disappearances what chance at dignity had the poor woman had?

On Friday, after eagerly anticipating their long drive alone into the city together, Heather was disappointed to find Zoltan in his overcourteous, icy mode, beginning the moment he entered the car. All across New Jersey their conversation was strained, with long patches of silence replacing their habitual playful banter. They spoke briefly about the color of the leaves along the highway, the environmental virtues of her hybrid car, the weather, but not a word about his weekend plans, which loudly lay between them unmentioned and unmentionable. Finally, as they were about to enter the Lincoln Tunnel, Heather couldn't take any more. "You've been awfully quiet today. Is something wrong, Zoltan?"

"No, no, it is nothing. I am most grateful that you are driving me in your Toyota Prius. It's New Jersey traffic—too crowded and slow."

Heather rolled her eyes. The traffic was as impersonal a topic as the weather.

When he asked her to drop him off at the Times Square subway station, she said, "That's not necessary. I'll take you wherever you want to go." But he insisted that Times Square was "exactly where I want to go."

"But Zoltan, you don't know the subways and I'm willing to drive you."

"No thank you. I do know the subways. I taught one semester at the New School, remember? Yes I need you, my darling, but not for *everything*."

"Fine! Our restaurant is in Hell's Kitchen. I'll park the car and you can go wherever you please."

As they left the garage, she had the feeling that he thought she planned to spy on him. Unfair! He was the one deceiving her and she was catching the blame. No kiss on the hand tonight, not even a wave, just a short, curt bow and good-bye. By the time they parted she was close to tears.

14 MACK, BARBARA, AND ABE Rabin were already seated at a table in the colorful main dining room, drinking mojitos, when Heather arrived. Rabin, a hefty man with a dense mane of prematurely gray hair, large moist hazel eyes magnified by thick glasses, and a muscular neck and double chin, stood up while cheek pecks and air kisses were exchanged all around.

"Where's the houseguest?" Barbara asked. "Mack said he was driving in with you."

"I dropped him at Times Square."

"Then he's not joining us?"

"He had another date," chirped Heather, trying to sound unperturbed.

"Too bad!" Barbara's disappointment was visible in the droop of her narrow shoulders and downturn of her full pretty lips, belying her usual offhand cool.

"He's spending the weekend in the city," offered Mack.

"Oh, really? With a woman?" asked Barbara.

"No. With friends of his, a couple named Shaffer," said Mack.

"I didn't know that," said Heather. Relieved, she hailed a passing waiter and ordered a margarita, then picked up the menu. "Does everybody know what they're having?"

For a while they concentrated on the menu, but once they'd placed their orders, the conversation returned to Zoltan.

"Frankly, I didn't really expect you to bring him," said Barbara. "Abe believes you want to keep him to yourself."

"No, you're wrong there," said Mack. "I invited him to come tonight. But Zoltan does whatever the hell he likes, regardless of what we might want. He's actually quite mysterious about his comings and goings."

"I'll say," said Heather, sipping her margarita. "I've never met anyone so secretive."

"Heather says he's difficult. What I want to know is *how* is he difficult?" asked Barbara, tapping a long silver fingernail against her glass.

"So many ways!" said Heather. "For one thing, he's a master of double messages. And contradictions. Like, he's stone broke but he brings us bottles of vintage wine. Or he needs every minute to work but he sleeps half the day. Or he longs to be part of a 'real family' but he can't remember the children's names. I think he snoops in our drawers when I'm out."

"How interesting! I wonder why," said Rabin, a psychiatrist, whose profession it was to wonder why.

"Oh, come now, Abe, you know why," said Barbara. "Writers are born snoops. They're always looking for material. They justify everything they do, no matter how bad, by telling themselves they're doing it for art, and then they use it in their books. They're shameless. Remember Henry James's prescription for writers? *Try to be one on whom nothing is lost.* If it has to do with their intimates or their family, so much the better, they think it rightfully belongs to them. And who knows, maybe they have a point."

"You two better watch yourselves or you'll wind up in a book," warned Rabin, wagging a plump finger. He picked up a chip, scooped up a large dollop of guacamole, and popped it in his mouth.

Unlike Heather, who sometimes feared being material for Zoltan, Mack harbored that very hope. "I'm not worried about it. He's asked me to be his business manager, so I expect I'll have a chance to vet his manuscript before anything damaging sees print."

"You don't get it," said Barbara. "Not even their editors have veto rights, only the lawyers, who can stop publication if necessary to prevent a lawsuit. They know how dangerous writers can be, even if you don't."

"Hardly more dangerous than developers," said Rabin, playfully punching Mack on the arm. "Look how many developers get indicted. Whereas the papers served to writers are mainly awards."

"Aren't you forgetting the libel suits?" said Barbara.

"And invasion of privacy," said Heather, licking salt from the rim of her glass.

"And plagiarism," said Mack. "If you ask Zoltan, though, it's not writers or developers, it's women who are the dangerous ones. He sometimes refers to Heather as a 'dangerous woman.' Though I think he means it as a compliment."

"He said that?" asked Heather brightly. "You never told me that."

"What he actually says, I believe, is that when I let you out of the kitchen you're dangerous."

"Then he's not worried that you'll poison him," said Rabin, filling another chip, this time with salsa.

Heather turned to Barbara for sympathy. "Once he said to me, 'With a kitchen like that I would think you would spend more time there.' Some of the things he says are unbelievable!"

"What a throwback! He's not the only Eastern European writer with old-fashioned ideas about women. Think Kundera. Does he ever offer to help you?" asked Barbara.

"Are you kidding? I doubt he'd know how. He acts completely helpless."

"Not when he's alone, I'll bet," said Rabin. "He's a bachelor isn't he? Bachelors have to eat too, so they can usually find their way around a kitchen. Unless they can afford to eat out every night."

"My impression," said Mack, "is that this bachelor has always had women to do his cooking."

"And he's quite particular about the food he eats, too. You could even say finicky," said Heather.

"Go on, babe," said Mack, grinning, "tell them about the strawberries."

"Ah yes, the strawberries." Heather drained her margarita glass and licked the last bit of salt from the rim, while the waiter set their entrees before them: beef fajitas, enchiladas with ground pepita sauce, and the house specialty, duck breast with mole negro.

"Well, after Zoltan had been with us a few days, Mack suggested I take him food shopping with me so I could find out what he likes to eat."

Mack interrupted: "He'd been barely eating, just picking at his food. He's thin as a rail to start with, so you can understand that I didn't want him wasting away on my watch."

"So I took him to Organic Eden, the best market in our area," continued Heather. "He pushed the cart through the aisles like it was some big novelty, picking out an item here or there, just like the children, until we reach the fruit section. Now he gets all excited. (Remember, he's just come from California.) Oh, what gorgeous strawberries! he says. How he loves them! He can't believe we have such big luscious strawberries on the East Coast when it's nearly winter.

"Of course, they were way overpriced, but since he made such a fuss about them I bought two boxes and for dessert I arranged them on a platter with some other fruit. He took some of everything— except strawberries. Take some strawberries, Zoltan, I said, I bought them specially for you. No thank you, he says, I'm allergic to strawberries. I couldn't believe it. But you told me you love them, I said, that's why I bought them. And he smiles his naughty-boy smile—show them, Mack—and says, yes, I do love them very much, but I cannot eat them, they give me hives and headaches."

Rabin slapped the table and laughed loudly. "Classic passive-aggressive behavior. If he wasn't famous he couldn't get away with that shit."

"See?" cried Heather. "Didn't I say he's trying to drive me crazy?"

Barbara pushed her glasses up onto her head where they rested securely in her thick black Afro. "So then what?"

"Then," said Mack, "our tough-broad Heather burst into tears right at the table."

"I don't believe it," said Barbara. "That's not Heather."

Heather shrugged her shoulders and shook her head. "I know it's not. But it may be soon. Because that is what I did. And probably not for the last time, either."

For a while the conversation turned to the Rabins' recent trip to Mexico. This mole, the Rabins agreed, though better than usual for New York, was not nearly as complex as the moles they'd regularly had in Oaxaca, which prides itself on having eight different classic mole sauces. Which somehow led Mack to speak of Zoltan's adventure with the starlet in Mexico, which led in turn to the subject of Maja's suicide, until once again Zoltan was in their midst, dominating the conversation.

"I'd be curious to meet him," said Rabin. "Interesting-sounding case. I'll also be curious to see how long you two can put up with him. It's not a good sign when someone's lover kills herself."

"I actually knew her fairly well," boasted Mack. "It was through her I met Zoltan. That suicide— I'm not sure it's fair to pin it on him. First of all, he wasn't her only lover by any means."

Heather could hardly believe what she was hearing. She put down her fork and stared at Mack.

"And remember my friend Terry?" continued Mack. "When he left her she tried to kill herself, too. In my opinion she was never all that stable. Complicated family, immigrant, troubled relationships with men."

While Mack paraded his expertise, Heather was quietly appalled that her husband had just admitted his own involvement with Maja—in front of not only his wife but also their closest friends.

"Of course suicide is never someone else's 'fault,'" said Rabin.

"As for our being able 'to put up with' Zoltan, as you say," continued Mack, "you're wrong, there, Rabin. True, he can be unpredictable, but he is also incredibly stimulating. He's like no one I've ever met. He's also been through a lot of bad stuff in his life—prison, exile, no money. I'm willing to give him the benefit of the doubt and chalk up his strangeness to cultural differences. Right now he needs us, and we're delighted to have him. Aren't we, Heather? Let him put us in his book if he wants to, I for one would be honored."

"All the same," said Rabin, "I'd advise you both to develop some defenses pretty soon. Especially Heather, since he seems to go after the ladies."

"Are there some pills you can prescribe for me, Rabin? No, don't laugh."

"Maybe an antistimulant?" quipped Barbara.

"You want to try some Xanax?" offered Rabin. "If you can wait, I've got a drawerful of samples of this and that in the office. Meanwhile . . ." He took a pen and prescription pad out of his pocket and began to write.

15   HEATHER HAD JUST RETURNED home after dropping the children at school when she was confronted by the ring of the phone. She flung her coat on the hall bench and dashed to get it.

A woman! A self-assured, husky-voiced woman asking for Zoltan.

Heather stiffened. "Who shall I say is calling?"

"Just say a friend."

She had a strong urge to tell that woman that Zoltan was writing now and could not be disturbed, but she didn't dare. She knocked on Zoltan's door and opened it. "Sorry to interrupt you, but you've got a phone call." Seeing him seated at the desk in his kimono, with the mussed, open bed behind him, she wondered if he had been in bed until hearing her drive up and only then, in order to deceive her, had rushed to the desk.

Zoltan followed Heather to the hall telephone. While he held the receiver to his ear, she busied herself straightening up in the vicinity. Ashamed to be hovering but too curious not to.

With his back to her he conducted the conversation in a low voice, then bent to write something on the blue notepad kept there for the purpose. As he tore off the note and thrust it into his pocket, she realized that in all the weeks she'd had him to herself, she had done little to secure her position. She had failed to see that it was only a matter of time until rivals would begin turning up. Without warning, time had turned against her. She imagined her advantage dissolving in a stream of phone calls from hopeful women: the artists and writers he'd known at the colony; aspiring students from the New School; editors, critics, literary groupies. Why hadn't she thought of them? One phone call and he was already acting like a cheating husband; if she didn't do something, he could start disappearing, like Mack.

"You're rather popular for a monk, aren't you?" she tossed at him.

"One phone call hardly makes one popular. Anyway, my darling, you are already taken."

"Be careful. I can be very jealous," she teased, pretending to be merely playing at jealousy. She offered to take messages for him instead of calling him to the phone, but he declined.

As she watched his tall frame recede toward his room she felt her hold on him—and on herself—slipping away with each step. If she didn't act quickly he would be lost to her.

Impulsively, with the nerve that had once prompted her, alone of all the girls in her entire high school class, to apply to Yale, coupled with the decisiveness Mack had modeled as a man of action, she stripped the band from her ponytail, shook out her hair, stepped out of her shoes, and followed him to his room.

When her knock drew no response, she turned the knob and opened the door.

Back in bed, a startled Zoltan clutched at the covers.

She took his return to bed for an invitation—what else could it mean? Hadn't he flirted with her shamelessly from the day he arrived, calling her *my dearest* and *my darling*, kissing her hands and cheeks at every opportunity, ravishing her with his eyes?

"I'm freezing," she said, sidling toward the bed. "May I?"

Before he could answer, she slipped in beside him and nestled her cheek against his naked chest.

Zoltan tensed. What was he to do? Here in his room that was really hers, she had every advantage.

She could hardly believe what she was doing. She was not herself. Or she was two selves at once. One of her, the cautious, cunning one, was appalled by the risk she was taking—to her dignity, her pride, her marriage—while the impetuous, infatuated one grabbed the opportunity and charged recklessly ahead. "Hold me," she whispered.

On his back, trapped, he lay awkwardly with one arm at his side squeezed between her thigh and his; when he finally extricated it, there was no place to put it but behind her neck, which forced him to turn toward her and accept her kiss. And how could he not return her kisses, stroke her perfumed hair, take her nipples between his lips when she opened her blouse? How could he not oblige?

She heaved and sighed. The long angular body of this mysterious man, with its black fur even on his thighs, was the antithesis of Mack's, a contrast that only intensified her desire. Whereas Mack's penis fit comfortably against her pelvis when they kissed, Zotan was so tall that his pressed exotically into her thigh. She wriggled down the length of him to take it into her mouth and possess him. Like his body, it was longer and thinner than Mack's. And shockingly uncircumsized.

He abandoned all resistance. Though this pleasure was surely forbidden, he remembered the loophole whereby in North America fellatio was not universally considered having sex. Yet when he closed his eyes in sweet submission, Mack's enormous leering face suddenly loomed overhead, like a Woody Allen mother, until Zoltan abandoned the distinction and went limp.

Heather redoubled her efforts, using advanced techniques, but to no avail.

He pushed her away and left the bed. "I'm afraid I can't."

She abruptly became herself again—the sensible one who could calculate consequences, make titillating small talk, maintain some self-control, for god's sake. She buttoned her blouse. However awkward or tense the situation, they were back to handling it with words. "Don't worry about it," she said encouragingly. "These things happen."

"Ah, my dearest Heather," he said, as he pulled on his kimono and sat down beside her. "You do not know me. I tried to make you understand, now I will try again." He took her hand in his and stroked it gently. "I went through very much turmoil in L.A., as Mack knows. It's why I left. If I am better now, it is because I am a monk."

There it was again. Monk. She thought of Thomas Merton, Savonarola. Neither image fit. What monk flirts so blatantly, or drives a woman to suicide? From the first moment he'd bent to kiss her hand and each time he'd fixed her in his powerful gaze it had been clear that he was no monk. Often she had seen his skin flush when she approached him, had felt him bristle when they touched, had recognized in him the same desire for her that she felt for him. Now too—his hand generated electricity. It couldn't be all pose.

"Are you saying," she ventured, "that you don't want me?"

He nodded.

What did he want, then? A woman like Maja? How had she behaved with him? Too bad she couldn't consult Mack. Of course, she and Maja were incommensurable, incomparable, every person was unique, just as Zoltan was nothing like any other man she'd ever encountered: he didn't sound like the others, with his strange accent and stilted speech; he didn't look like them, with his scarecrow frame on which absurd costumes hung awkwardly; and, helpless as a child in the face of necessities, least of all did he act like them. She couldn't imagine him wrestling with food or laundry, technology or taxes, though he was already middle-aged. What did he do when he had to find a doctor, buy a ticket, sew a button, play a video? He needed the help of someone like her. As he walked away from her toward the window fussing with his sash, pulling it ever tighter, she searched for a reason he would refuse her offer of so much that he needed. "Is it that you don't find me attractive?" she forced herself to ask.

He tossed his black lock off his forehead and scanned her with glittering eyes. "Certainly not! You are a devilishly attractive woman. It is not you, I assure you. It is I. I am . . . unable." He spread his hands imploringly. "You understand?"

Heather wondered if Zoltan's inability was a matter of will, like a monk's, or some problem beyond his control. "Do you mean it's something physical?"

He wished he could tell her exactly how physical his problem was: as physical as room and board. "Let us say . . . psychological. Where there is woman there is also conflict."

"But you were able with Maja, right?"

He raised a hand. "Please do not bring up Maja. You cannot understand. That relationship was very complicated."

"But that's just it," said Heather, assuming the voice of reason. "With us, it wouldn't be complicated at all. It would be simple. We're alone together here every day and we find each other 'devilishly attractive.' What could be simpler than that?"

"Your husband," he chided her. "It is he who invited me here."

"Let's leave Mack out of it, too, then," she returned. She wondered why, if the two men had no problem sharing Maja, Zoltan was making such a fuss about sharing her. "He doesn't have to know anything about it."

Zoltan looked out the window to conceal his dismay. A wind was whipping the trees, sending leaves whirling into the air. Heather was like a high wind, a tornado, blowing in to make him homeless. He stopped to compose himself. "Now, let me try to understand. You propose that we, that I, that you and I—" He shook his head. The situation was completely untenable. Not that he cared that much about violating the so-called sacred bonds of matrimony, but hospitality and loyalty among comrades were, if not sacred, at least deserving of respect. He cleared his throat and started over. "Let me understand. You are proposing we have an adulterous affair right under your husband's roof?"

"Actually," she said, smiling wryly, "it's my roof, if you want to get technical. The house is in my name."

He raised an eyebrow. "Pardon me, I had an impression that you and Mack were happily married." Even as he said it he knew how fatuous it sounded. The myth of the happily married. But then, how should he, happily single, be expected to know about married life?

"If we were, do you think Mack would have invited you to live with us?"

"Perhaps I am . . . naive. Mack did say . . . He gave me an impression this marriage was . . . well . . . different."

Heather bit back Maja's name. Did Zoltan believe that a happily married man would take, to use his word, a mistress? Everyone thought their own marriage was different. She'd thought so too. Now she wondered how to overcome the handicap of *difference*.

"Why *did* he invite me?"

Heather smiled. "Maybe he invited you for me."

Zoltan shook his head in disbelief. "For you?"

"Well, for himself, then. In case you haven't noticed, Mack likes power. Having you here gives him a chance to parade as a powerful, generous man.

He *is* a powerful, generous man. And he likes to make me happy."

Zoltan could not decide which Mack deserved more: pity or contempt. "Then your wanting someone to talk to was only—"

"No. It's absolutely true. Until you arrived I'd practically forgotten what it was like to have a genuinely interesting conversation. I treasure our talks. They're so stimulating that they've stimulated me to want more."

"More than this?" he asked, sweeping the room with his arm.

She followed his glance to the beams, the hillside, the woods. "Oh, yes, it is beautiful here, and much more peaceful than in the city, plus all the advantages for the children. But it doesn't talk."

Everything Heather said plunged Zoltan deeper into confusion. He feared that her eyes, bright with passion, would fill up and overflow again. The tears he had found charming his first night in this house now seemed as dangerous as Maja's. Were all women the same? What he needed was solitude; what she needed was company: irreconcilable differences. She was daily becoming less fascinating and more terrifying, like a North American Madame Bovary: self-destructive, incapable of foresight, in

love with danger, willing, like their legislators, gov-
ernors, and presidents, their Kennedys, Spitzers,
and Clintons, to spoil everything for a foolish
affair. "What exactly is it you want?" he asked
gloomily.

It was the other Heather, the impulsive, besot-
ted one, who met his eyes. Exhilarated by her own
daring she answered recklessly, "I want you."

16   JAMIE WAS ON HIS way to the bathroom from the playroom, where he and his sister had been cutting construction paper into scary shapes while Carmela cleaned around them, when he heard the hall phone ring. As instructed, he waited till the third ring before picking up. "McKay residence. Who's this?" he said.

"Hi Jamie. It's Daddy."

"Hi Daddy! It's Jamie! Where are you, anyway?"

"Right now I'm in the middle of Manhattan driving in vicious traffic. What are you doing?"

"I'm talking on the cordless phone."

"You certainly are, James my boy," said Mack, charmed. "Is Mommy there?"

"I think so."

"Could you give her the phone please?"

"I'll try—but I can't if she's with Zoltan."

Mack's curiosity stirred. "Why not? Is she in his room?" When Jamie didn't answer, he said, "Do me a favor, buddy, okay? Go see if she's in his room. Could you please do that for me? I'll wait."

Jamie bounded up the stairs toward the study carrying the phone, then tiptoed to the door of Zoltan's room. Unable to knock for fear of Zoltan's stern staring eyes and incomprehensible speech, he stood there bravely for a while listening at the door. No sound emerged. "Daddy?" he whispered into the phone. "I don't think anybody's in there."

"Did you knock?"

"No."

"Try."

After a silence, he said, close to tears, "I can't, Daddy."

"Okay, never mind. Try Mommy's office. Or the kitchen. I'll wait."

Released from his burden, Jamie tore down the stairs, calling "Mommy! Mommy!" When he reached the room that now served as her office the door was closed, and again he hesitated to knock, not because he was afraid of his mother as he was of Zoltan but because he wasn't supposed to interrupt her when she was working unless it was important.

He considered. What could be more important than his father's command? Nothing, he decided, and knocked.

Dressed in turquoise sweats and a matching fleece jacket, Heather sat on the outside deck of the room she had taken as her office, leaning against the house, with laptop in lap, while Tina watched her regally from atop the railing, tracking her every movement with her unblinking eyes. Since Zoltan's arrival, Heather's fantasies had so pressed against reality, and the days had tumbled by so quickly, that without her noticing, the deadline for her column was looming, and she had barely begun it. Now she was furiously trying to catch up.

Startled by the knock, thinking it Zoltan, she called, "Come on in. I'm out here." When the door opened a crack, it was Jamie's small head peeking through.

"Daddy! I found her!" he said triumphantly into the phone. "She's on the deck."

"Good work, James." Mack was relieved that she was not upstairs bothering Zoltan, whose comfort he considered his responsibility.

Jamie went through the room and tugged open the sliding door to the deck where his mother, smiling, beckoned to him. "Here. It's Daddy," he said proudly, handing her the phone. Mission accomplished. Tina took the opportunity to slip through the open door into the house.

"Thank you, sweetheart." Heather tousled his curly hair. "Hello? Mack?"

"I'm so glad you're there, babe. I was starting to worry."

"But why? I'm always here, you know that. I'm not the one who disappears."

A mistake; an opening he should not have given her. "I only meant I didn't know where you were, since you didn't answer the phone."

"I've been working on the deck since lunch, so I didn't hear it ring. I find I suddenly have a deadline. What's up?"

"I'm afraid I'm running late again, babe. I'm stuck here in traffic, so I don't know when I'll get home. I'll try to make it to dinner, but don't count on me."

There they were again, those familiar stomach-churning words that she could never get used to no matter how often she heard them. But though she felt the usual sinking disappointment, this time it was balanced by the equally elevating prospect of an intimate dinner with Zoltan. Which of the feelings was stronger she could no more say than she could tell which image, a pair of profiles or a vase, the famous optical puzzle depicted. Each depended on the other, and no sooner did she focus on one than the other snapped unbidden into view.

"Oops, another call coming in," said Mack. "Love you, babe."

She pressed OFF and handed Jamie the phone. "Will you be my big helper-man and hang this up for me? I'm going to finish this one paragraph and then I'll come up. If you like, you and Chloe can play in the kitchen garden, where I can see you while I get your dinner." Before she could manage to kiss him he was running down the stairs off the deck. "The phone!" she called after him. "Don't forget to hang up the phone."

Jamie hit his head and made a silly face, then raced back up the stairs, across the deck, and into the house, leaving Heather to slide the door closed after him.

SIPPING WINE AND NIBBLING olives at the kitchen table, Zoltan looked out the window to see the girl raking dead leaves into piles on which the boy was stomping, leaving the earth with both feet at once. One moment this Breughelesque autumn pastoral,

and the next moment Heather, who had been filling the children's plates with food prepared earlier
by Carmela, was flying out the door. He watched her
snatch up a rake from the leaves, then hug the girl.
The enchanting sight of mother and children romping in the windswept yard excited him, making it
hard to believe that the serpent in this Eden might
be Eve herself, conniving to get them both kicked out.

It wouldn't happen if he could help it. That afternoon he'd conceived a plan, a plea bargain, to
enable them to live out their sentence in peace. In
the brief moments she was outside he went over his
pitch once more.

She returned flushed and breathless. "One of
them could have punctured a foot on that rake, or
worse yet, the handle could have snapped up and
hit someone in the head. Or the eye." She covered
her eyes and winced.

"I see. Another dangerous weapon," said Zoltan
slyly. "But sit down Heather, please. I wish to make
a proposal."

As she took a seat, he switched on the brights in
his eyes.

"This morning you said that you *want me*?"

She winced again. What madness could have
possessed her? Although she was now half ashamed

of the entire brazen encounter, at this moment she was too curious about where the conversation might lead to deny or explain away her words.

"Then my darling you shall have me. All parts of me I am able to give."

Had he forgiven her, then? Either that or he had never truly objected. "And which parts might those be?" she asked, relaxing.

He stood up behind her chair, placed his hands on her shoulders, and began gently kneading the muscles and vertebrae. "Listen carefully. What I say now is important. You know I have made a monk's vow against sex and writer's vow of discipline. That is why I left California, that is why I came here. It is my highest priority. But—" He stilled his hands. "If vows are fulfilled I can be yours."

When he resumed massaging her shoulders, she leaned back into his hands and closed her eyes.

"Six hours a day I work, no interruption, no distraction. Distraction is most dangerous tyrant to depose and slay. Distraction will drive me away."

Heather stiffened. According to Mack, it was Maja's constant distraction that made Zoltan dump her.

"But," he continued, "after those six hours, I can be yours." He moved his hands to her arms and bent his mouth to her ear. "Our consummation will be spiritual, not carnal. That is better, you will see. The Dalai Lama has said that in order to achieve subtlest levels of consciousness the rougher levels must cease, that when sexual energy is controlled, as in tantric practice, subtler levels become active. Of course, that requires much concentration and control, but if successful, the superior bliss of true spiritual union can be ours."

Could that explain it then? she wondered. Could that morning's apparent ineptitude have actually resulted from discipline and control? Is that what he meant by "monk"—some California thing to enhance pleasure that he was now offering to bring her in on? She wanted to believe in it, though at the same time she wondered if the spiritual consummation he was promoting wasn't just a cover-up for his failure.

He dropped his voice to a trancelike purr and returned his hands to her shoulders, then down her upper arms, sometimes brushing with the lightest touch against the sides of her breasts. She felt her nipples stiffen through her T-shirt.

He continued: "During the day, you and I in a spiritual marriage. But at night we will be one family—you, me, Mack—not of blood, but of affinity. Elective affinities."

Could that be what had gone on between Zoltan, Mack, and Maja? she wondered.

"Family of affinity," he repeated, moving his hands down to massage her ribs.

Once more she relaxed into it, like a dog being stroked by its master—tongue lolling, legs in the air. Her breath grew regular, her lips parted, her eyes fluttered closed. She could hardly believe the turn things had taken, the pleasure and relief she felt. One minute disgraced, and the next full of hope again.

A late-night movie she once saw played in her mind: two people meet in a diner, fall instantly in love, and plot to murder the woman's husband, whose only fault is being in their way. What made the movie so terrifying was the way the outcome of the story was foregone from the moment the lovers laid eyes on each other. One look, one word, and everything followed. Like Lot's wife, turning back for one forbidden look at the burning city of Sodom only to become a pillar of salt. For eternity. Heather did not want to be Lot's wife. She didn't want to look back or become a pillar of salt. She wanted to move fluidly forward, become something new, extraordinary . . .

Perhaps this feeling was what he meant by spiritual bliss.

At last Zoltan pressed his palms to her ears and kissed her chastely on the crown of her head. "You are fascinating woman, as Mack says."

"'Quite a number,' I think you told him."

He laughed. "Quite a number, yes."

"But 'dangerous,' you also said."

"Very dangerous."

At that moment a drumroll of children burst through the kitchen door. Seeing Zoltan bent over their mother, they stopped their forward lunge until he moved aside, giving them an unobstructed shot. Heather's euphoria spilled over her squealing pups, now tumbling into her open arms and onto her lap.

Zoltan took the moment to pick up his glass and slip out of the kitchen. He had managed to pacify her, but could it last? It was entirely possible that their sexless truce would only renew her desires or stir up new ones.

If he hoped to live here as a free man perhaps the time had come to speak to Mack.

17 ZOLTAN STOOD IN THE doorway of Heather's makeshift downstairs office wearing a brown tweed jacket, tan shirt, and black string tie, over his usual black jeans and scuffed shoes. His hair, which had not been cut since he'd moved east, grazed his shoulders.

Heather was alarmed. "Why the getup? Where are you going?"

"To Manhattan."

She stood and circled him, tilting her head in mock appraisal, while he squared his shoulders and pulled at his tie. He looked even more exotic to her in his not-quite-business clothes than he did in his Mephisto garb, like an actor turned magazine salesman. Falling into their new parody of marriage, she straightened his collar, turned him around, smoothed the fabric of his jacket across his shoulders, picked at lint.

"I don't know, Zoltan. Are you trying to pass for someone else?" How she wished he would offer to tell her where he was going and with whom, so she wouldn't have to ask! But he offered nothing, forcing her hand. "May I ask who you're meeting?"

Zoltan stiffened. She had no right to ask him that. She was not his mother. More like his jailer. As it happened, he was meeting an agent referred by a friend. There was no reason such a meeting should arouse Heather's jealousy, although it seemed everything did. But as he wanted to avoid setting a precedent, he remained silent for what seemed a full minute before giving in. "I am meeting an agent. Mack will bring me home."

Heather was dumbfounded. Why hadn't Mack mentioned it? She wondered whether this agent was a woman—maybe the one who had phoned, maybe someone unsuspected.

"I'll drive you to the station."

Or maybe he was lying to her and not meeting an agent at all. If so, how was Mack involved? Perhaps Zoltan's move east was less innocent than they let on; maybe Maja was not dead after all but instead ensconced in a Manhattan flat alternately receiving Heather's two men. Maybe that was why Zoltan wouldn't fuck her. Who, she suddenly wondered, was deceiving whom?

As soon as Zoltan disappeared inside the station she felt abandoned. It was the first time that he had gone off and left her behind. When each of her children had started preschool she'd also felt bereft, though at the same time joyously free; she had celebrated her freedom by taking her first freelance job. Now she felt only forsaken.

After lunch, while the children were drawing and coloring in the playroom, Heather took a sponge and a rag to her—now Zoltan's—study. With Carmela out sick, she had a perfect excuse. She had not crossed the threshold of the room since the day of her botched seduction (as she thought of it), although she had sometimes listened at the door.

Throwing open the door, she saw that much had been changed: furniture had been repositioned, pictures moved, books rearranged. She read each change as a clue—as if the room were a poem whose meaning was traceable through its several drafts. He had pushed the sofa bed toward one wall—to command a better view? She looked out the window trying to capture the inspiration for the sake of which he had violated the room's symmetry. The laptop she had lent him was no longer on the desk but sat on a table near the window with her old printer. Neglected flowers, parched in barely an inch of scum-covered water, drooped their heads toward the table, now dusted with the fine yellow powder of their withered stamens. She blew it to the floor. Running her cloth across the shelves, she studied the book titles for illumination. Wherever she looked papers and folders greeted her—proof of the creative life that flourished inside this room while her own creative life was on hold.

She ran hot water in the bathroom sink and scrubbed the porcelain with a sudsy sponge. Zoltan's toothbrush—a sad specimen, with splayed bristles that had lost all spring—aroused her pity; but then, she reminded herself, he had called himself a monk and chose to ignore his body. She folded the crumpled towels, lifted each of the odd bottles on the sill to wipe the woodwork underneath. Opening his aftershave, she found herself breathing in his singular astringent aroma. She glanced inside the medicine cabinet at a cryptic array of pills and salves; but though she examined them closely, searching for clues to maladies, she could not extract their secrets. Nor did the act of dusting the chair he sat in or wiping away his fingerprints land her any closer to the mysteries of his life. He sat writing in this room; he crumpled up sheets of paper; he read, he thought, he slept—and he went out.

She carried the overflowing wastebasket to the utility room and was about to empty it into the appropriate recycle bin when her eye caught a scrap of blue paper bordered in green—a page from the notepad she kept beside the telephone. Discarded trash could hardly claim privacy rights. She straightened it out and read: E.—Thu 1, Endicott lobby.

Today was Thursday!

She recrumpled and discarded the note and without a scruple picked up another sheet—this one of lined legal paper covered in cramped vertical script—and began to read.

"PLEASE HAVE A SEAT and I'll tell Mr. McKay you're here," said the sloe-eyed receptionist through glossy puffed lips.

Zoltan eased himself down onto a low sofa. The reception area was as refined and comfortable as a living room: a small, finely worked prayer rug, visible on the floor through a glass-topped coffee table around which stood two modern sofas covered in velour, compelled his admiration. The warm rusts and reds, the deep blues, the intricate pattern of curves and leaves distracted him from the heavy feeling he carried of being utterly displaced. His clothes, his posture, his very thoughts affronted the elegance of this anteroom of commerce. In place of the highbrow journals and literary reviews casually displayed at their mountain home, here recent copies of *Time*, *Fortune*, *Contemporary Architecture*, *BusinessWeek* were arranged on two side tables in crisp symmetrical groupings. He flipped through the pages of *Fortune* observing the square-jawed, tailored, muscular American men.

"Hey, Z," said a grinning Mack, extending his hand. "You managed to find your way. Come on back to my office. I have a couple of things to finish up and then I'll be ready to go. Ruthie dear, could you please call down and ask them to bring up my car?"

As soon as Ruthie left, Mack looked Zoltan over. "You know, Z, I'm not sure about that tie, or the jacket either. I mean for seeing agents and such. Maybe okay for L.A., but you're here now, you might as well look it. Don't you agree?"

Zoltan bowed. "You are my business adviser, I follow your advice."

"Good. Tomorrow we'll go shopping. I'll come home a little early. There's an outlet store just across the highway. We'll surprise Heather. But you better not pull that shit you pulled with the strawberries. If I buy it, you wear it."

"That was entirely a misunderstanding. I do love strawberries. I only—"

"Forget it." Mack waved it away and opened the door to his office. "When she sees you in your new duds all will be forgiven. She'll be so jealous."

"Jealous? Why jealous?" Exactly how much, wondered Zoltan, did Mack know?

"Because she didn't get to pick them out herself. But tell me, how did things go with that agent?"

"I will tell you in the car."

He followed Mack into a spacious room furnished even more like a living room than was the reception area. A few papers and catalogues were piled neatly upon a large walnut dining table, which served as a desk. While Mack typed on the computer, Zoltan sat down on a graceful loveseat and looked around. The floor was decorated with more Persian rugs and the walls with framed photos of spectacular buildings going back to the Parthenon.

The large windows gave out on the phallic tops of skyscrapers against a puffy blue-and-white Manhattan sky. If there were files or drawing boards or equipment, they were hidden behind the paneling that covered one entire wall; only an elaborate phone and the large computer betrayed any sign that this luxurious room was indeed an office.

Mack hit ENTER with a flourish and turned to Zoltan. "What do you think?"

"Very impressive, very impressive," muttered Zoltan. "I especially admire your rugs."

"Rugs, nothing. Come over here if you want to be impressed." Mack led Zoltan to the window, elevated over the city like a throne. Below and beyond them spread a vast peaked range of roofs and spires, dotted with conical shingled water towers like native huts, stretching to the east and west, down to the rivers. Sunlight danced on metal, gleamed off glass. "It always amazes me how almost delicate the tops of the old skyscrapers are. Look at that one over there," said Mack, pointing to the graceful, silver tower of the Chrysler Building a little to the south of them, seemingly at eye level with their window. "What an achievement! It's not only the shape that gets me, but all that decorative detail— put right up here in the middle of the sky. When that building went up no one could have expected it to be visible at close enough range to be appreciated. It was done for the sheer beauty of it. That's some inspiration for a builder, isn't it? Someone poured a lot of love into that project. Each morning when I come in, I try to start off the day by contemplating those stainless steel scalloped arches just to remind myself that nothing I ever do can match that."

Again, Zoltan felt the power of Mack's ambition surging behind his humble words. Some minutes later, in the car, this impression built momentum. The more gently, humbly, Mack spoke, the more aggressively he drove—gunning at the lights, weaving in and out of traffic, and then, after they left the city, speeding on the highway as if driving were a race and its goal to overtake the greatest number of moving vehicles—while Zoltan, seat belt fastened, sat tense and helpless in the passenger seat.

HEATHER LOOKED AT HER watch. The children, off on a school trip, would be home soon, and the men were probably heading home. Sitting in the utility room among the recycle bins, garden tools, nature bowl, and newts' terrarium, she'd been so intrigued by Zoltan's crumpled pages that she'd lost track of the time.

No wonder identity thieves searched the Dumpsters! No telling what fascinating information you could glean from the trash. Except for the telltale blue note, she'd found no other clues to Zoltan's personal life, no names of dates besides E, not a mention of Maja. Yet studying the discarded pages yielded revelations no less valuable. Since Carmela had last emptied his wastebasket he'd evidently reworked and discarded the same basic paragraphs repeatedly, with only small variations and no discernible progress. What a surprising glimpse of the creative process of a genius! Both as an editor and as a writer she appreciated the necessity of refining the work; but at this rate, how would Zoltan ever finish anything? And why did he continue to write in longhand when he had access to an up-to-date laptop? In her search for clues to his achievement, instead she discovered in his tortured process a spark of hope for herself. She was probably deluding herself, but by comparison her own writing seemed crisp and efficient.

She stood up and dumped Zoltan's trash in the mixed-paper bin. To hide the evidence, she added a pile of her own office trash and topped it off with discarded scraps of construction paper from the playroom. Then she hurried to the kitchen.

"SO TELL ME," ASKED Mack, when they were out of the tunnel, "how'd the meeting go with the agent?"

"She likes my idea but needs to see more pages before she can commit."

"Well, can't you give her some then?"

"Not yet."

Mack scowled. "Maybe I'm out of line here, Z, but as your business adviser I wonder why the hell not?"

Zoltan stiffened. "I don't have any yet ready to show."

"But why not? You've been working for weeks now. Tell me—aren't the working conditions satisfactory?"

Zoltan glowered, irritated and amazed at Mack's complete ignorance of an artist's needs and pressures. As Maja would say, his cluelessness—as clueless in his way as Maja. Perhaps he should never have expected better of a man like Mack. How could such a man, who toppled mountains, comprehend a writer's ambivalence and hesitation, much less writer's block? Still, Mack's question could be the opening he'd hoped for; he swallowed hard and leaped. "No, no, my room is perfect. But—well, actually, the problem is more about privacy."

"The kids making too much noise? Are we—"

"No, no, no. Noise does not bother me. Kids are practically invisible." The authority Zoltan commanded through eye contact was worthless here, with Mack concentrating on the road. He lowered his voice. "May I speak to you frankly, Mack?"

Just what Mack had been hungering for. Another dose of man-to-man, like that first exalted night of confession in L.A. "Shoot."

"It's your wife."

Mack checked him with a fast glance. He'd never expected things to go perfectly, not with a woman like Heather, who had her own agenda. But he hadn't expected her to fuck things up, either. Having Zoltan Barbu in residence was as much a coup for her as it was for Mack—and not one he was ready to give up. The leverage of having a wife like Heather—not only beautiful and talented but peppery, bold, unpredictable—had to be constantly balanced against the potential disruption. He'd briefly considered the possibility that her discontent would tempt her to go too far and seduce their guest but decided it more likely that Zoltan would go after her. Discontented or not, she had far too much to lose if she messed up, even more than he had. Still, Zoltan's arrival had whipped up in her a gale of feelings he considered it his duty as a husband to monitor. Sometimes he couldn't tell if she was crying or laughing; her sleep was turbulent and erratic; she was all paradox. If diplomacy failed and the worst did happen, if they actually launched an affair behind his back, he liked to think he was big enough to handle it. "What's the problem? She interrupts you?"

"Not exactly. She is actually rather scrupulous about rules. I assure you, Mack, I hope to give you everything you want from me, but I suspect she wants something I am not able, or not prepared, to give her."

"Which is . . . ?"

Zoltan had resolved to confine himself to speaking generally, working in only such details as might be required to show his good faith, his loyalty. "Shall we say, attention? Certain kind of attention. She is so . . . restless, you could say, so . . . distracting. Even with door closed I feel her there behind it watching me. Makes concentration very difficult. I expect this surprises you. I hope it does not also upset you, my man."

Mack slapped Zoltan lightly on the knee, hoping to appear relaxed. "I know what you mean, Z. Frankly, I have the same feeling about Heather myself sometimes—even when I'm hundreds of miles away. But you—in the house with her all day—it's got to be worse. What would you like me to do about it? Formulate a comprehensive privacy policy with an opt-out option?" Seeing Zoltan straight-faced, he chuckled to indicate: joke. "Seriously, though, would you like me to talk to her?"

"Whatever you think. She's your wife."

As pivotal person, air traffic controller, Mack felt reassured. Zoltan would hardly be complaining if they were fooling around. Since he was complaining about something, Mack took it upon himself to reassure him. Whatever was needed to keep him from bolting. "I know she doesn't want to interfere with your work or upset you. She means well. She just happens to be one of those women who always manage to make their presence felt—know what I mean?"

"I suppose that is one way of saying," said Zoltan, raising an eyebrow.

"Try to look at it her way. As she sees it, it's her house, she's in charge of it, you're both there all day long, so she keeps an eye on you. As she does on the kids. I'm sure she's only trying to be useful—you can understand that, can't you? Maybe if you could indulge her a little—"

"I don't see why she needs my indulgence when she obviously has so much of yours."

"Ah," said Mack, with dawning comprehension, "you think she's making a play for you. No, no, no, don't deny it. I'm sure you're getting mixed messages at the very least. But I know Heather. She may be coming on to you, but believe me, all she really wants is a certain amount of appreciation. She's a woman, remember. Naturally, your work must come first, we all know that. But it probably wouldn't take much time to give her a bit of intellectual companionship. Talk to her about your work. Your friends. Your past. The political situation back there. Talk about books—you see how she loves books. Take her into your confidence. If you lighten up a little she probably will too. All she really needs is to feel special."

Zoltan had been prepared for several responses from Mack—anger, gratitude, dismissal, even love—but nothing had prepared him for this closing of ranks, this all-out spousal support, elevating marriage *über alles*. It made no sense. No marriage did, but especially this one, which imposed upon him an impossible dilemma: to satisfy the wife without betraying the husband, to honor the husband without enraging the wife. He was beginning to think it could not be done. Unlike Heather, who acted as if it were possible to serve two masters, he knew it was not.

"Hold on tight," said Mack, shifting down. "We're going up."

18 IT STARTED WITH PHONE calls— always polite, at decent hours, people with unfamiliar voices and sometimes vaguely familiar names asking please to speak to Zoltan. Then one day he turned up with a cell phone, and from then on Heather felt cut out. Cut. Out. After that at any time of day or night she might hear the low murmur of his voice, laughing, purring, or holding forth, behind the closed door of his room.

The honeymoon was over.

She was in the kitchen chopping onions the first time Zoltan announced to her that he would not be home for dinner. Afraid he might attribute her tears and sniffles to something other than onion fumes, she stood with her back to him and continued to chop until he took the knife from her hand, laid it down, grasped her shoulders, and turned her around.

She gasped. Before her stood an unimaginably dashing Zoltan in a new suit (black of course), pale peach shirt, elegant tie, even shiny new shoes. And his hair! Except for the long forelock, it was now shorter than on the day he arrived and stylishly cut.

"Courtesy Mack. You like?" he asked. He pulled her toward him and, singing loudly in a foreign tongue, whirled her around in a parody of a waltz.

"Zoltan, stop it!" she cried, pulling away. Not for her had he decked himself out like Dorian Gray. Why had Mack done this to her? She drove Zoltan to the station in silence.

The next day, hoping to pacify her, as Mack had advised, Zoltan appeared suddenly at the door of Heather's office to announce that he had brought her a surprise from Manhattan.

"What?" she asked, softening.

"It's a surprise. Please wait five minutes, then I will call you."

He hurried to the kitchen. From a bag he took a jar of pitted lychee nuts and dished them into two small bowls. After setting the table with spoons and napkins he summoned her.

"Please, sit," he said with a sweeping bow.

She looked skeptically at the four strange translucent balls floating in her dish in a pale yellow liquid. "What is this?"

"First, taste."

Zoltan spent a gleeful moment watching her raise her spoon to her lips, chew thoughtfully, and swallow the first ball. "You like?"

"Kind of. It has an odd texture but it's sweet. What is it?"

He leaned forward, twinkling. "You want me to tell you?"

"Yes."

With a wild grin he cried, "Is the eyes of a large animal of my country, like moose. You don't have them in America. For us they are rare delicacy."

"Eyes! Gross!"

He threw back his head with a roar of laughter. "What is the problem, you don't like?"

"Come on, Zoltan. Tell me the truth. What are they really?"

But he would not change his story. "Delicious," he said, taking a spoonful of the syrup and smacking his lips.

"You're just like Jamie!" she said suddenly, and in a moment, she couldn't help herself, she was laughing too. Which she did again every time he lifted her hair and whispered into her ear in a certain way his native word for "eye." Even when he began to miss her dinners two, three, sometimes four nights a week, plunging her into a sullen gloom, he could usually manage to raise a laugh from her by bending down and whispering the mysterious word into her hungry ear.

Mack was not inclined to laugh at the turn things had taken. Not that he didn't welcome the occasional respite from their two- and three-o'clock bedtimes so they could catch up on their decimated sleep. He sometimes felt so exhausted that his bones ached. But he didn't like what Zoltan's absence was doing to his wife. His own frequent absences, which couldn't be helped, upset her enough; he had invited Zoltan here in part to fill that void, in any case, to make it better, not worse. Yet worse seemed to be exactly where they were. He knew it was necessary for Zoltan to seclude himself in his room to write his book, but at night? Gallivanting around Manhattan at night was not part of the deal. The more Zoltan stayed away, the more moody Heather became. Mack felt responsible for her misery, as if, having given her Zoltan, he ought also to have prevented his defection, which filled the air like smoke, leaving a thin film of ash on everything, including their former pleasures. It wasn't only on the nights Zoltan was absent that he saw Heather suffer; on the nights he graced their table it was hardly better. If he evaded their questions about his whereabouts she felt rebuffed; if he filled them in on his excursions, she felt excluded. Mack wished he could sweep her off to Harbor Island or St. Barts for a few days in the sun, but with upcoming trips to Chicago, Boston, and L.A., he couldn't possibly spare the time.

Feeling the strain, Zoltan did his best to soothe his hosts. He quoted Molière and Nietzsche, Plato and Proudhon, made frequent enigmatic pronouncements, and the next time he dined with them at home he presented them with an excellent bottle of Pomerol.

"Hey, Heather! Look what Z brought us," beamed Mack. He clasped Zoltan's arms and said, "Good job, Z. How did you know this is one of my favorite wines?"

Zoltan knew because the bottle came from Mack's own cellar. Though he could not disclose this, that very morning, while Heather was delivering the children to school, he had extracted it from one of three cases of the same vintage stored in the pantry, confident that one bottle among so many would not be missed. He had been regularly slipping out more modest wines to present to his other hostesses, and no one had noticed. Even if his prank should eventually be discovered, it would be Mack's responsibility, not his. Mack wished him to indulge Heather? Then he would indulge her and assume Mack would appreciate his efforts.

As it happened, the Pomerol was exactly right for the duck breast Heather served, garnished with apples, on the Spode plates, as the centerpiece of that particular dinner, and they polished off the bottle just before dessert. Dessert was another triumph (prepared by Carmela, but still): a crisp made with newly ripened apples from the McKays' own trees. Earlier, from his window, Zoltan had seen Heather and the children tramping off to the woods with a pole and buckets to collect them. Remembering his own boyhood pleasure in gathering windfall apples on his way home from school or choir practice as an offering to his mother, he'd briefly considered abandoning his (anyway futile) work for an hour or so to join the pretty family group, only to quash the impulse on second thought. Although in principle he appreciated children as much as the next man, in practice he felt awkward around them, a limitation he presumed would disappear should he someday produce his own. He supposed the McKay children were charming enough, but he was always glad when Heather or Carmela gave them their dinner in the kitchen in advance of the adults, making it easier for him to entertain his expectant hosts.

When the meal was finished and the men were seated in their usual places in the living room, Mack took two cigars from his pocket, handed one to Zoltan, and said expansively, "You know, Z, you don't always have to go to the city to see your friends. You're welcome to invite them up here if you like. Put on some music, open some wine, make a fire."

Zoltan had come to this sanctuary to write, not to socialize. But he could not escape the conflict that dogged him wherever he went. In L.A. it was the movie crowd that seduced him from work; in New York there were the literary distractions. Naturally, it soothed his vanity to be publicly esteemed, if only for his early work, the new edition of which sported an appreciative preface by his MacDowell lover, Rebecca Shaffer; still, the backbiting rivalry that ruled New York was bad for his stomach and his sleep. Not only strawberries but other writers gave him headaches. No, he would never foul his

Eden by bringing his rivals here; better to pacify the McKays by taking them there.

Mack continued. "We'd be glad to pick them up at the station, or if you prefer, you could use one of the cars yourself. We wouldn't intrude."

Across the room Heather, who had been just about to pour brandy, froze. Intrude—in her own house? Had she heard Mack correctly? What was the matter with him! She waited for Zoltan to demur, to say that of course they should join them, but instead he leaned into Mack's proffered match and puffed.

"Very kind of you, my man," he said when he was lit, "but I must decline . . ."

"Think it over," said Mack magnanimously, after lighting his own cigar. "Might as well take advantage of all this space."

Heather was flabbergasted. The two of them! She tried to catch Mack's eye, but he was too busy bonding to glance her way. Would either of these men, their heads clouded in smoke, egging each other on, give a thought to her? She had gladly rearranged her life to accommodate Mack's whim. And after Zoltan had moved in, she had devoted herself to him. For him she had sent Françoise back to Belgium, tabled her work, compromised her security, deceived her husband, even lied to her children. And when he had refused her his body, declaring himself a monk, she had accepted his terms, maternalizing herself to serve him: she dispensed advice, kept the children quiet, tailored her menus to his taste, became his laptop consultant and his chauffeur. But absent herself in her own house while he entertained? Somewhere she had to draw a line.

"Funny you suggest this now, when I also have invitation for you," said Zoltan, and he proceeded to invite the McKays to a holiday book party for Orville Lask at the Manhattan home of the literary critic and hostess Rebecca Shaffer. "That is, if you are free to come one week from Saturday."

"We're not free," said Mack, "and neither are you. We're all going to *Der Rosenkavalier* that night, don't you remember?"

"Ah . . . yes. But afterward?"

Heather considered it a fault of her essential Midwestern optimism that she was never able to hold on to anger in the face of any reasonable excuse to drop it. Now in the warmth of Zoltan's invitation her resentment began to melt until, relieved of its burden, she forgave him, forgave them both. "Thank you, Zoltan," she said, genuinely moved, despite a small residue of skepticism. And presenting him the opportunity to prove himself, she added sweetly, "But you really don't have to invite us. We could just drop you off at the party after the opera."

Loyal Tina leaped into her lap and began to purr. She stroked the sleek gray fur as she waited to see what Zoltan would say.

"No, it will be my honor. Rebecca particularly asked me to invite you." ("Zoltan," Rebecca had admonished, "you must bring along this mythical couple you say have adopted you so I will know what powers can trump mine." "But my darling, you are married." "And they are not?") "There will be many people you might enjoy. If not, we leave."

After their big Kansas wedding, the McKays had returned to Manhattan, where Heather worked in a midtown office a few blocks from Mack's, two subway stops from their new apartment. Full of plans, they had set out to create for themselves a certain kind of ideal urban marriage modeled on images of New York life they'd read about or viewed, they couldn't have said exactly where. Each week they scanned the reviews in the *Times* and the cultural listings in the *New Yorker* and *New York Magazine* before buying tickets to enticing events; sometimes they invited along another couple—the Rabins, or people they had known at school or met through work, people who had similar tastes or whom they told each other they wanted to know better—going out afterward to a restaurant for a late supper or down to a club in the East Village. They had taken buses and taxis, learning the differences between Szechuan, Shanghai, and Hong Kong cuisine, Northern and provincial Italian cooking, going with the crowds to the special exhibitions at the big museums and with the strays to cult movies, and to Central Park on weekends, until Mack began his rise and Heather became pregnant with Chloe. Then they had moved.

Although several times a year they were still invited to a party of some old friend from their city days or for drinks with one or another of Mack's business acquaintances who lived in Manhattan, or, now that Mack's name was getting known, to various testimonial dinners, literary parties like Rebecca Shaffer's were out of their reach. "You see?" said Mack, squeezing Heather's arm as they headed downstairs to bed. "He's opening up to us. I knew he would. It's just taken him a while to get going."

"Maybe you're right," said Heather. "We'll soon see."

She couldn't tell anymore whose side Mack was on. He claimed to be her ally and champion, but when it came to Zoltan, there was some inscrutable connection between them that made ally sometimes feel more like adversary. Had it been forged over Maja's body or was it a fallback to primitive male bonding? Whatever it was, she sometimes felt trapped in a buddy movie.

While she changed for bed in her dressing room, Mack, who was leaving for Chicago in the morning, began to pack.

"Have you seen my good cufflinks? I can't find them," he called from the closet.

"Did you look in your top drawer?"

"They're not there."

Heather slipped into her nightgown and went to the closet to search. "Maybe you left them in one of your shirts," she suggested.

"Diamond cufflinks? I don't think so."

She began systematically employing the technique she'd developed for helping the children find lost things. "Okay, then, when did you last see them?"

"You don't suppose Carmela—"

"How can you even think that!" Heather broke in. She couldn't bear to mistrust Carmela, whose affection and skill with the children were indispensable, now that Françoise was gone. She didn't want to suspect Zoltan either, or it would all be over. "Françoise is a likelier candidate, she had nothing to lose when she left the country."

"No, I wore them to a benefit two weeks ago; long after Françoise left."

"What shirt were you wearing? Maybe they're still in your cuffs."

"How can I possibly remember that?" he snapped. He picked out a pair of opal links to take instead, and after locking the jewelry drawer, added the key to his key ring rather than hanging it back on the door. He then locked Heather's drawer and handed her the key to hide.

"I'm sure they'll turn up," Heather consoled him, concealing her key among her bras. "And if not, we're insured."

It was after one when they got into bed. Seeing Mack's long-lashed eyes unfocused without their contacts and his solid neck naked on the pillow, Heather thought how vulnerable he was under his powerful facade. Touching, sometimes surprisingly tender, and vulnerable. With the edge of the top sheet she carefully wiped a trace of toothpaste from his lips before kissing him good night and extinguishing the light. "Love you, babe," he mumbled, snuggling against her. Large wet flakes of snow, like rolled oats, floated past the window in a slow-motion free fall. She was glad to be warmed by Mack's thick, comforting body, so unconcerned about what was coming that it was already heavy with sleep. She herself was madly curious. She wanted to peer ahead, as she often did in a book, to see what was going to happen. But it was the wrong metaphor for her life. In real life, there was no way to preview what was in store. Supposing you could somehow steal a peek, it still wouldn't help you, because event followed event with such gal-loping speed and necessity that until it was over, you could barely reflect upon it, much less alter it. No accidents.

19   THE ELEVATOR OPENED DIRECTLY into the small entrance area of a huge, high-ceilinged loft. A plump woman held out both dimpled hands to the McKays and both rouged cheeks to Zoltan, then pulled them all into the main room. She smelled of jasmine, and throughout Zoltan's introductions of the McKays to their hostess she flashed perfect white teeth.

"So you're the lucky people Zoltan has settled in with," said Rebecca Shaffer, flushed with the reflected glow of purple silk and polished hardwood floors. "I'm so glad to meet you, finally. Put your coats back there in the bedroom. Zoltan can introduce you around."

Her age was indecipherable, but Heather guessed she was probably in her mid-forties. She had the unlined luminous skin that often served as consolation to the fat; her delicate mouth and nose were diminutive and shapely amid the rounded cheeks and chins. Nevertheless, Heather was astonished that a woman of such girth, despite the power that came from writing reviews for the *Times* and *New Republic*, had attracted literary lovers of the stature Zoltan had intimated.

"Intimated? Are you kidding?" said Mack. "She probably broadcasts it."

"Do you think that Zoltan—?"

"How would I know. Maybe." Then the lovely Maja crossed his mind, and he revised his judgment. "No, I wouldn't think so. Highly unlikely."

Fluted cast-iron columns painted mauve held up a stamped tin ceiling crossed with sprinklers and pipes; not even the crush of cruising bodies obscured the spectacular wall of windows facing south toward all the lit-up towers of Lower Manhattan and the harbor. To Heather, this loft defined a life, one she had let slip away with hardly a fight, like so many others: the small studio with fireplace and Murphy bed and dainty furniture somewhere in the West Village where she would live alone; the rollicking punk pad (her hair spiked and wild); a summer cottage by a lake, half of it a kitchen, with fishing for the children; this loft. On their way to the bar she whispered to Mack, "Wouldn't you love to live here?"

He stopped short. "Are you kidding? Trade what we've got for bare pipes and sprinklers? With exposures like these, this place is a furnace in the summer, unless you seal all the windows and air-condition every last cubic inch. Count 'em. Then imagine the bill, with these high ceilings. Plus, nowhere for the kids to play, no windows in the bedroom, city noise and fumes—you'd hate it here, believe me. You've got such romantic ideas, Heather."

Other people, she brooded, did it and loved it and went on excursions to the mountains or the beach in the hot summer. But she supposed he was right; this was what he knew best. Still, if Mack died, she would sell the house and live off the proceeds—buy herself a loft, eat brunches at Balthazar, shop at the Farmers' Market, cruise the Chelsea galleries.

"Besides," continued Mack, stomping her dream, "this would cost us twice as much for a fraction of the space we've got now. Real estate markets all over the country are tanking, but Manhattan prices stay astronomical. And what have you got when you're through? Essentially one big room. For singles, maybe; for a family, forget it."

"Okay, okay."

Heather spotted Zoltan near the bar talking to two attractive people: a man whose bald (or shaved?) head was firmly set atop a youthful body sheathed in jeans, Western boots, and a dark, well-tailored jacket; and a young moon-faced woman painted with a slightly garish shade of blush and style of eye treatment. She was wearing one of the two uniforms of the season—cashmere-and-silk top with dark, skinny pants, or else a short black sheath. Suddenly, scanning the room, Heather feared she herself might be the only woman in the entire place wearing a party dress. She blushed.

Zoltan waved the McKays over. He'd been told to take care of them, introduce them around. "Come, Heather, Mack. I want you to meet Wayne Auerbach and . . . ?"

"Ericka Esposito," said Wayne. "Zoltan Barbu."

"Oh," said Ericka, catching her breath, "I've heard of you."

"These are the McKays, Heather and Mack," continued Zoltan. "My benefactors."

Heather took Zoltan's arm in one of hers, Mack's in the other, and announced they had just come from the opera, hoping to explain her dress.

When she looked down she saw Mack's missing cufflinks in Zoltan's cuffs.

Barely glancing at the McKays, Ericka focused her blue gaze on Zoltan. A string of round blue beads around her neck matched her large, almond-shaped eyes. She wore her beige cashmere top tucked into a strikingly slender waistband, with a silk scarf tied in an artful French knot at her throat. In an excited voice she exclaimed like a child, "You're famous, aren't you?"

Wayne coughed; Zoltan puckered his lips into the smirk he wore to denote modesty (what was he to say? Thank you very much? No I'm not? It means nothing? You may be too, someday?) and proceeded with the introductions. "Wayne here, famous New York editor. Mack, famous builder. You should see the Eden we live in that he built."

"Really? Where?"

"In Wildbloom, New Jersey."

"New Jersey!" said Ericka, shocked.

"There, there, my dear," said Wayne, patting her hand, "contrary to recent studies, there is still life beyond Manhattan and Brooklyn."

"We are exactly seventy minutes from Lincoln Center," defended Heather.

"And we have a forest in front yard," added Zoltan, rewarding the McKays with the unexpected "we."

"And a river," added Mack.

"And books. Walls and walls of books. Heather has amazing library," said Zoltan.

Heather beamed for her books.

"Really? Then as soon as you get home you should look up Chekhov's *The Seagull*," said Wayne. "Or perhaps you remember? Act II opens with Irina and the doctor reading Maupassant. Now pay attention to this, Ericka. 'It's as inadvisable for people in society to fawn over writers and invite them into their houses as for a corn chandler to raise rats in his granary.' Who should know better than Maupassant or Chekhov?" He grinned like such a rat. "Consider yourself warned."

Chagrined by Wayne's patronizing remark, Ericka turned to Heather for relief. "Are you a writer too?" she began. During the introductions, the women's occupations, unlike the men's, had not been specified.

"No. Well, yes, if journalism counts. I write a column for *EarthBell*, the online journal? And you? Are you a writer?"

"I wish! I'm a reader, though," said Ericka, bobbing her head, as the three men drifted off with their drinks. "I haven't read anything he's written, but now that I've met him I'm going straight out and get his books."

She paused to pluck a piece of tekka maki from a platter held by a passing blonde in a black tux, and for the first time Ericka's initial registered on Heather. Could she be the E-person Zoltan had met for lunch? Could they be deceiving her with this sham of being strangers? For all his penetrating glances and intimations of intimacy, Zoltan was as secretive about his life as a spy, rendering every woman here a potential rival.

"What's it like living with him?"

Heather laughed a proprietary laugh. "Sometimes it's like having an extra child in the family—although we do have some very unchildlike conversations."

"Does he show you what he's working on?"

"Not exactly. But sometimes he talks about his writing."

"If he was living with me, I'd read his manuscripts when he went out. But you won't tell him I said so, will you?" She giggled, crinkling her blue eyes and covering her mouth.

Near a corner table Mack popped raw cashews one at a time into his open mouth and watched the guests circulate among the writers positioned like pillars around the room. He watched and popped until the bowl was empty. "Here, let me fill that up," said Rebecca, the hostess, sidling up from behind, reaching for the empty bowl.

"Not for me," said Mack, "I've had enough."

"Don't be silly, There's no such thing as enough," she said, followed by a brazen pause. "So, I hear you've built yourself quite a dream palace. Zoltan says it's a writer's paradise. Makes me wonder if we shouldn't have been less rigid about leaving the city."

"You've got a great place here. Must be a hundred people, and it doesn't even feel crowded."

"Yes, it's a lot of space for the city, but I'll bet this whole loft would fit into a little corner of your flower garden. Am I right?"

"Oh, I don't know. You can't really compare a loft like this with a house in the country. Most of our garden, as you call it, is Ha-Ha Land."

"Ha-Ha Land?"

"Wilderness owned by the state."

"All the better. Taxes will pay the gardener. I guess everything is a trade-off. We've got twenty-four-hour delis in every direction, while you've got nature. And Zoltan."

Mack laughed. "You think Zoltan wouldn't prefer to live in the city if someone offered him a place?"

"Oh, I know he wouldn't. All the frenetic fuss of city life is just what he doesn't want right now. He's desperate to write, and he says your place is ideal, a private artists' colony. He told me that if he can't write there he'll give up trying."

Mack wondered why, in that case, he was so seldom home nowadays.

"We can't get over how nice you were to take him in, flat broke, practically a stranger," continued Rebecca. "For someone with his talent for getting into impossible situations, he finally seems to be doing something right. Personally, I think you're probably the best thing that could have happened to him—a stable family situation. I want you to know I am personally very grateful to you."

Mack thought it odd that Zoltan had hardly ever mentioned this woman who spoke as if she owned him. She began to seem less fat and more voluptuous; he would have to read her stuff.

"I was thinking of giving a party in honor of Zoltan's return to New York, but since he's described your estate, some of us were hoping that maybe you'd want to have the party instead. Do you think I'm naughty to suggest it?"

Something in the way she said the word "naughty" gave Mack the distinct impression that she was suggesting more than he could make out. Heather called him naive about women, "a pushover." He remembered other parties where women had asked him things he didn't know how to answer, and Heather, ever alert, had had to interpret for him afterward. "No harm in suggesting," said Mack. He thought he was saying it noncommittally, but the particular laugh Rebecca tossed at him, her head cocked coquettishly, her lips parted to reveal the iridescent teeth, told him he might have conveyed something more. She took his arm. "Come. We're both empty. Let's fill up together."

Over Ericka's shoulder Heather watched plump Rebecca pirouette before Mack, then steer him to the bar. Women liked her husband—friendly, generous. He was the man who remembered your birthday, your drink, your favorite song, your best color, the man who offered to take you up in a plane or help you with onerous tasks like packing and moving, who had things shipped for you and got things wholesale, who picked up the check, who drove home anyone who asked, the farther out of his way, the better. Heather knew these qualities were simply pufferies of ego and said nothing, but she took note, kept track. If Ericka had to be watched, then so did Rebecca.

Orville Lask, the guest of honor, clasped both of Zoltan's hands. They had first met at a writer's conference in Santa Fe and then wound up sharing an office at the New School. He was small and sickly, with a perpetual sniffle, a high voice, flat feet, and rimless glasses, whose career had been devoted to developing in print an image of himself as big and tough, as his enemies were quick to point out. He did not resemble the picture on his book jackets. Before he and Zoltan had become office mates, he had twice written pointed criticisms of Zoltan: once for his long silence and once for his "sententious" style; but today he could afford to be chummy, not only because he had excluded those particular essays from his new collection, but also because this was his book party and, unlike Zoltan and all the other writers present who weren't publishing anything this season, he was relieved of writing worries while he was occupied promoting his new book and a few grace months more.

"Rebecca tells me," said Orville to Zoltan, "you've got yourself another setup. Rich patron, dream house in the country. Son of a bitch, you always did know how to pull off deals, didn't you?"

"What do you mean?"

"Don't be coy. You know what I mean. Hollywood contracts, free pad in the Village, now this. Bet you're banging the wife, too?"

"Be careful," said Zoltan, "she's standing right there. And, no."

"Where?"

"There. In the green dress."

"Damn! Is there some foundation to apply to?" Zoltan smiled.

"When you get tired of country living, man, introduce me, okay?"

A waiter carrying a platter of puff pastries topped with crabmeat caught Zoltan's attention. He bowed slightly before following the waiter, who was now a few steps away. He snatched up a canapé and slipped it whole into his mouth. He was just settling in to chew it when a stranger pronounced his name.

"Zoltan Barbu?"

Annoyed to be interrupted before having a chance to fully savor the canapé, Zoltan examined the person's face: stuck-out ears, moist, bulbous eyes, a high forehead that would have excited a phrenologist, a stringy neck circled by a bow tie.

"Tony Agasian," said the man, extending his hand. "I thought that might be you. We met years ago at the Aspen Institute, on a panel on Writers in Exile? Remember? But what are you doing here? I thought you were in California writing for the movies."

Zoltan swallowed. As he was systematically searching his memory bank, Agasian sprang on him the Forbidden Question: "So what are you working on?"

Zoltan was aghast at such a breach of etiquette. Writers had been known to choke on their food or spill their drinks in face of such a blatant demand to justify themselves. Those who could brag of a recent success or a book in press were exempt, but everyone else felt assaulted by the intrusion. Even the phenomenally prolific John Updike once confessed in print to resenting it; how much more so the bulk of writers who exerted their maximum labors to produce one or two books in a decade. On the early advice of a friend, Zoltan had prepared a response to the Question, especially when asked by a layman—which presumably described this meddling Mr. Agasian. Either that or, if he too was a writer, he was perhaps a sufferer of Asperger's syndrome, a major symptom of which was a lack of empathy and social grace.

Before Zoltan could deliver his rehearsed response—I am currently working on a very long project that I am not at liberty to discuss—his interlocutor's cell phone began playing Beethoven, and he gestured to be excused.

With relief, Zoltan moved quickly away. The decibel level of the room was high enough to give him a headache; big parties always brought back to him the inescapable noise of prison. As he made his way toward an open window, he spotted a clutch of people who had been at MacDowell with him and Rebecca. (Did she stay in touch with everyone she ever knew? Was that the secret of her social success?) Among them was Sophie something, an up-and-coming poet who had been working on her second collection. At the first composers' recital in the colony library she had come on to him by inviting him to visit her studio for "tea," but the timing was wrong; Rebecca had two more weeks left at the colony, and by the time she was gone Sophie had hooked up with someone else. Tonight she looked better than he remembered. He quickly searched the room for Heather before approaching her but was stopped abruptly by the insistent ring of silver spoon on crystal goblet, wielded by Rebecca, who thwarted him once again.

"People! People! I have an announcement," she shouted, flanked by her tall, hunky neurosurgeon of a husband.

People began exchanging signs. Zoltan swiveled in his tracks and urgently searched for Mack, to signal his desire to leave.

"I am so glad that you could all join us tonight to tip a glass to our guest of honor, my dear friend Orville Lask, one of our most distinguished public intellectuals, who has kindly agreed to grace us with a brief reading from his new book, published just last week."

There was a sudden scurry of bodies as some claimed choice seats on one of the leather sofas or grabbed a chair, while others began inching toward the coatroom.

Rebecca continued: "This book is bound to make an important contribution to the cultural life of our city, in fact the debates have already begun, as you will see in next week's *Times Book Review* . . . Yes! Isn't it wonderful? A page four review! And no, I did not write it; we are far too good friends. This is the *Times*, not *n+1*." (Laughter.) "But don't take my word for it, you will see for yourself. Now, if you'd like to refresh your drinks before Orville begins . . ."

Mack, who had just emerged from the bathroom, caught Zoltan's signal and went immediately to the bedroom to retrieve the coats while

Heather, flushed with happiness, picked up the signal from across the room and went to summon the
elevator. In the few moments between Rebecca's
finishing and Orville's beginning to speak, Zoltan
commandeered his hostess's hand for a parting kiss
intended to convey their regrets at being unable to
stay for the reading and discussion. Rebecca shook
a remonstrative index finger at her "naughty boy"
but in the end relented, bestowing on him her signature white, coy, sparkling, flirtatious smile.

Zoltan hurried to the elevator. Rebecca, performing magical action at a distance, zinged her
smile across the room to dazzle the departing three
before they were swallowed by the elevator doors,
then swiveled to beam it on the waiting guest of
honor.

THAT NIGHT, WHILE MACK punctuated boozy sleep
with loud apneatic snorts, Heather, still high on
the party but brought low by its revelations, lay
awake reeling between hope and resignation,
gratitude and defeat. Just like college, where the
triumph of being at Yale was marred by the humiliation of being treated like a coed—two sides
of a single experience she could not reconcile. Her

parents were so proud of her being there that she couldn't admit her distress even to herself; instead she became engaged soon after graduation, taking the easy out. Throughout the party she'd been swamped by double messages, unable to tell if she and Mack were more envied, pitied, or scorned. At the very moment Zoltan seemed ready to include them in his glamorous life, she got a glimpse of the formidable competition ranged against her.

The next day she could hardly wait to ask Zoltan about Mack's cufflinks. When she did, he shrugged it off as if it were nothing. "Shirts Mack bought me have cuff holes but no links. So I borrowed Mack's."

"You just opened his drawer and took them?"

"What could I do? He was not home. Is there problem?"

"No, except he had no idea where they were. He thought maybe they'd been stolen. You could have mentioned it."

"Stolen! By thieves!" he said sarcastically, widening his eyes in mock alarm. "I tried to put back, but drawer was locked, key gone. Mack has many cufflinks. Does he need also those?"

"I'll say this for you, Zoltan. You've got great taste. You took his best pair. They're diamonds."

Zoltan stuck out his lower lip. "Proudhon says property is theft."

Heather could only shake her head.

"Give me key and I will change them for others."

"No, you give me the cufflinks and I'll do it."

"Why?" he said, feigning innocence. "Mack says I should treat this house as mine."

"Including the contents? Come on, Zoltan, at least you should ask before you borrow something precious."

"You mean," Zoltan whispered, bending to brush her ear with his lips, "like his precious wife?"

20 "THIS IS NOTHING BUT a mess of disorganized notes, some letters, and maybe a couple of chapters at best," sputtered Mack, swatting the top paper on the pile with the back of his hand. "Where's the book?"

Heather shrugged. "Good question. There are hardly any traces of it anymore in the trash. Maybe it's on the computer. Maybe he doesn't print out."

"Impossible. These things are printed out."

"Then maybe he— Wait!" Heather cocked her head, but decided the shrill cry was only a blue jay, not one of the children after all. She didn't want them to discover their parents rummaging in Zoltan's room. Not that there was much danger of their mentioning it to him, since he never spoke to them. But why take a chance? She considered it her right, in the course of cleaning up, to glance at the screen of the laptop or to peruse the papers lying bare and unprotected on the table or tossed out in the trash. But, so far, she'd drawn the line at opening an envelope or a drawer. Mack had no such scruples.

"Let's hurry up, okay?" said Heather.

"Don't be silly. He's gone to stay with—what's that name again?"

That name, which Zoltan had surrendered to Heather only reluctantly, was seared into her mind in bold caps. "Elaine. Glinka."

"Well, he's not coming back until tomorrow. And whose house is this anyway?" Mack's only regret was having waited so long to investigate. "Look at these. He keeps writing to editors asking for advance money. Bad planning. While he's living here for free, he should stop worrying about money and just write. Unless," said Mack, recalling the unproduced screenplays, the spent advances, "he didn't really come here to write at all."

"Of course he did. I know for a fact he used to work on his book, because I found crumpled-up scenes in his wastebasket. But now that he's got that *girlfriend*"—Heather spat out the word as if it were spoiled fish—"he's never home, so how can he possibly write a book? Or even letters."

Things were not working out as Mack had planned. The happiness Zoltan had offered them hadn't materialized; Heather was plainly in a state, and Mack too had little to show for his trouble. The gregarious houseguest of the early weeks had morphed into a sullen adolescent. Was this a taste of what awaited them when their kids matured?

"How do you know they were scenes?"

"You can tell—descriptions, snippets of dialogue. I'm talking about the pages that were in English. There was also stuff in other languages that I have no idea about."

"Other languages? For all we know he could be a foreign agent or a spy. Even a terrorist. Maybe he was never a writer at all, maybe he just plagiarized some poor Balkan schnook."

"Come on, Mack. If he were a spy, wouldn't he know his way around a computer? He needs way too much help for a spy."

"Don't laugh, Heather. If he were a spy, that would explain a lot."

"Like what?"

"Like his sneaking in and out. His unbelievable secretiveness. Those surreptitious phone calls at all hours. The fact that he seems to do almost nothing. Another thing—why didn't I think of this before?—he asked me to give him flying lessons. Flying lessons!"

"Oh Mack, that could be perfectly innocent."

"Yes, but it might not be. And remember, he served time in prison. How do we know there wasn't some secret deal to let him out?"

"Come on, you know he was jailed because of his book. Of course he's a writer."

"Okay, maybe so, but so what? Look at all those first-rate German writers who it turned out were keeping dossiers on their friends for the Stasi. Maybe he has some secret arrangement with the CIA or the FBI. They hire the shadiest characters as informers."

Heather rolled her eyes, but Mack still wanted to know: was there a book or wasn't there? If not, then Zoltan, not Mack, was the impostor.

He began searching the drawers. "There must be a manuscript here somewhere. Whenever I ask him how the work is going he says it's coming along fine. Why would he lie about it? Why would he waste this perfect setup? Unless he is something other than he pretends."

"Maybe he took his manuscript over to *Elaine's*." (Poison word!)

"Do you know his password? Can you get into this laptop?"

"Of course I can. It's my laptop and my password."

"Okay. Boot it up."

Heather sat down at Zoltan's (that is, her) desk, opened the laptop, logged on, and surveyed the list of folders. Then she opened up the documents folder.

"Here's a folder for *Realms of Night*." She clicked on it. "Look how small the files are. Some are thirty kilobytes. And how few of them."

"What's this?" said Mack, pointing over her shoulder to a folder named "Projects & Prospects." "Open it. Or better yet, move over and let me."

He practically shoved her out of the way in his determination to get at the screen. The folder in question contained half a dozen files: one named Writing Projects, another named Titles, one marked Names (with subheads, male and female), a list of Publishing Contacts, another of Women, one of Sources, and one headed Housing, with annotated entries for artists' colonies, house sits, and various people. He ran his eye down the screen, then stopped. "Look, Heather! Here we are."

Heather followed Mack's finger to their names and read across: "Bourg lux, priv bth, vu 2 hrs nyc free bd, stipend." Below was a cryptic note that read, "pot dang sit."

"'Pot dang sit.' What the hell does that mean?" asked Mack.

"That's what I'd like to know," said Heather. Then in a flash it hit her. Suddenly nervous about what else Mack might discover about the *potentially dangerous situation* if this impromptu search continued, she looked up and said, "Did you hear that?" Tina, who had been washing herself on the windowsill, looked up too.

"What?"

"Didn't you hear something? Could be Chloe. Would you mind checking on them, please?"

"In a minute," said Mack, tapping his index finger on the screen. "This stipend business—what's that about? Stipend from whom, do you suppose?"

Heather took a deep breath and like a threatened head of state launched her distracting attack. "From you I suppose, who else? Haven't you given him money?"

"I sent him a couple of C-notes with his ticket from L.A., and every so often I slip him a few more. I did tell him not to worry about cash. But no stipend. And oh, yes, I gave him a check for that political foundation of his."

"What political foundation?"

"You know, the Fund for Balkan Freedom—something like that. The FBF or BFF. Didn't he hit you up too?"

"I think he mentioned it once. I thought it was Baltic, not Balkan."

"Baltic, Balkan . . . maybe it's a front," said Mack, scrolling down and down until he found a file labeled "$." "Look here. Here's a page headed FBF with an entry for two thousand dollars from me, and here's one for a thou from Paul Shaffer."

"Did he give you a receipt?"

"If he's a spy or this is some kind of scam you wouldn't expect him to give out receipts, now, would you? Anyway I have the canceled check. I could look up the endorsement. If it's a legitimate foundation, some officer other than Zoltan would have endorsed it."

"Come on, Mack, you know no one but Zoltan endorsed that check. He's the only Balkan or Baltic whose freedom counts here. No wonder he can take so many taxis from the station. Taxis, cufflinks, money—what else does he take? He takes and takes and gives nothing back. When he's here he barely comes out of his room, he hardly speaks a word to me anymore, the children no longer know he lives here. What a joke! I hear him talking on his cell half the day, and he stays out all night. He comes home in a taxi to shower and pick up his mail and goes right to sleep. Since he spends half his nights at his girlfriend's place anyway, since he's practically living there now, let her cook for him. Let him move his stuff out of here and give me back my study."

Glad to be getting some sleep again, Mack didn't really care where Zoltan spent his nights. But when he thought of the nonexistent manuscript and that "stipend" business he felt duped.

"Wait," said Heather. "I really did hear something. I'm going to check on the children. Right back."

As soon as Heather left the room, Mack, following an intuition, reached into the back of the top drawer and pulled out a small maroon notebook written mainly in a foreign script. Seeing dates in the margins as he turned the pages, he thought it must be some sort of diary and, feeling diaries were out of bounds, suffered his first small qualm. But when he saw "McK" sprinkled here and there with an occasional English word or phrase in quotation marks ("finance/build," "Eve in Eden," "enterprising as hell"), curiosity trumped qualm. Either this was some kind of spy journal or Z was taking notes on them. When Heather came back into the room he shoved the notebook in his pocket to study later.

"Heather, I've made up my mind. I think it's time we had a talk with him. Ask him about this so-called book of his."

"You know he'll just talk his way around it, so why bother asking? Look, Mack, he had his chance and he blew it. We should just tell him it hasn't worked out and ask him to go."

Mack hated failure almost as much as he loved success. "We can't just kick him out without notice. Just when he's beginning to feel at home."

"He'll never feel at home. Ask him. He says he's a permanent exile and can't feel at home anywhere."

If Zoltan was planning to write about him, Mack didn't want to act precipitously. "What if there is a book somewhere after all? And a Balkan fund. We could at least show him the courtesy of asking."

"Courtesy! Does he show us any courtesy?" Feeling herself once more on the verge of tears—whether of disappointment, hurt, or anger she didn't know—she turned to the window with her back to Mack until the feeling passed. She missed her room, her view, especially at this hour when the fading light turned the woods melancholy. When she trusted her voice again she said, "Go ahead and ask him if you want. But you know he'll concoct some story to make you do what he wants. Just the way he did in California. That's how he is. He gets his way."

Mack remembered their night together at the beach and that it was actually Mack's idea for

Zoltan to come stay with them, not the other way around. Heather didn't know what she was talking about.

"And you know what?" continued Heather. "Even if there is a manuscript somewhere, and a legitimate fund too, three months is long enough. Don't you think we've done our turn? Let him find his own place now."

"With what, babe? Be realistic. He has no money."

"Then how come he buys expensive wines and takes all those taxis? He must have some money. If he isn't getting it from you he's getting it from—"

"His handler?" quipped Mack.

"Let him start spending his money on rent. Or move in with his girlfriend. Or go down his Prospects list. Or get a job."

"Maybe the manuscript's with some agent or editor—"

"Didn't he plan to discuss it with you before showing it to anyone? Mack, think about it. You're probably right and there is no manuscript. Anyway, not enough of one to sell."

"All the same," said Mack.

"Look," she said with urgency, "we agreed he'd stay only as long as I want him. I don't want him anymore."

21 ZOLTAN HAD EXPECTED TO slip into his room undetected, but Heather was waiting for him in the hall. Caught. "Ah. Good morning," he said, backing away.

"If you like—though it's technically afternoon. It'll soon be time for the children's baths."

He was amazed at how presumptuously she regarded his comings and goings, as if he were another of her children.

She followed him into his room. Tina followed her and leaped up beside her as soon as she sat down on the folded-up sofa. While Zoltan stood at the window summoning strategies for getting rid of her, she lit one of his cigarettes and announced that she had decided to ask him to leave.

At first he didn't understand her. But seeing the cocky tilt to her head he divined her meaning. "Leave? You mean, move?"

"Yes." She blew out a long stream of smoke.

"You cannot be serious."

"I am, though." She smiled with satisfaction and curled herself into the corner of the sofa, drawing her legs up under her, just as she used to do before he had banished (or abandoned) her. For the first time since he had come to live with them she felt confident.

"When?"

"As soon as you can."

"But . . . why?"

"Did you think you could live here forever?"

"It's only been three months."

Would she dare to say it? She dared. "I'm afraid, Zoltan, you no longer charm me."

He raised an eyebrow at her, smiling, as if at some private joke between them. "And for that you would evict me?"

"You'd expect me to keep you? As if we were married?"

"I would hope so," he said, falling into their private banter.

"You're a cheating husband," she countered. For a moment his hair glowed in backlight, as the sun struck the top of the mountain before sliding behind, and she felt a stab of regret. She softened slightly. "Let's just say it's not working out the way we expected, okay? We gave it a good try, but it didn't work. You're not a monk, I'm not a saint. So we'll just go back to how it was before you came."

"Excuse me. Maybe you can go back, but is not so easy for me. I have no place to go."

Here was the cue for her best line; she launched it like a smart bomb. "Move in with Elaine, then."

He whirled around to stare at her.

Bull's-eye!

He sat down at the desk and drummed his fingers on the edge. "You cannot be serious," he repeated with an expression of such incredulity that Heather was momentarily taken aback by her own audacity.

She managed to hold on to it. "Why not?"

"Well . . . ," he stammered, "well, . . . I know Elaine a short time only. Never have we spoken of living together."

"You moved in here before you knew me at all. No problem then, right?" she tossed out cockily.

"That was different."

"How?"

Zoltan got up and began to pace from the window to the door and back again, a large trapped animal, as he had on her first visit to him in this room.

"Relax," she said. "I don't mean you have to move out today. You can take your time."

"Why, thank you, madam," he said with a sweeping bow. "But it is not only a question of time. Maybe I do not want to live with Elaine. Or Elaine with me. That is a very serious decision, you know, to live with someone. I cannot say that I am ready."

Heather shrugged and stroked Tina's back all the way up to the electric tip of her tail. "To tell you the truth, Zoltan, I sort of feel the same way myself."

They stared at each other in silence. Zoltan concentrated his eye power until Heather backed down. "Anyway, I'm not sure I believe you. You've been staying there practically every night for weeks; you've almost moved in with her already. It's only a matter of moving your things over too."

Zoltan was overwhelmed by her cunning, her blatant exaggeration. How did she know where he slept? But he would not lower himself to dispute the count with her. He sat down again and swiveled the chair around. "I do not stay there often. Her place is too small. Two tiny rooms. In any case, she would not agree."

"Why don't you ask her?"

Speechless, he stared at Heather. Then he repeated, "You cannot be serious."

Each time he said it Heather felt more certain. "Yes, I'm afraid I am."

"But why? What have I done?"

"Let's say it's more"—she looked at him defiantly and slowly exhaled smoke—"what you haven't done."

"Are you actually suggesting that if I, if we—" He closed his lips, his eyes. The gall of the woman! Sitting there calmly smoking and petting her cat, she seemed to him truly monstrous. First for what she did to her husband, now for what she was doing to him. An evil monster with ice green eyes.

"Frankly, Zoltan, we feel exploited by you. I kept my part of the bargain, but you haven't kept yours. You didn't come through for me."

"What do you mean?" Would she have the nerve to say it?

"I'm no less lonely than when you came. Certainly more stressed. I don't see why I should have all the trouble it takes to keep you when you give us nothing in return."

"I don't see that I am so much trouble. Often I'm not even here."

"That," she said, crushing out the cigarette, "is precisely the point."

He shook his head. "I can't believe you are sitting here saying these words. Suppose Mack knew?"

She smiled sweetly. "He does know."

"What does he know?"

"He knows that I am asking you to leave."

Zoltan looked around his room. He should never have allowed himself to become attached to this place. The perfection of this setting should have tipped him off; he should have known as soon as he saw the shameless luxury that there'd be a heavy price. His destiny was exile; one exploiter was the same as the next. The humiliation of being at the mercy of everyone with more money than he had. And now, how obviously she was enjoying herself! If he were Mack, he'd know how to deal with her. But Mack was weak. Behind all that bravado he was a wimp.

"When do you want me to go?" he asked with forced politeness.

She wanted him gone now, yesterday! But her heart softened. "I don't want to make it hard for you. Take as much time as you need."

Agitated, he resumed his pacing. He would leave tonight, sleep on someone's sofa, on a park bench, anywhere, rather than submit to the abjections, the humiliations of this arrogant bitch. Maybe Elaine would take him for a day or two while he tried to figure out where to go.

His mouth went dry, he felt his eyes burning in their sockets. He resumed strumming his fingers on the desk. Self-control. "Mack knows you are kicking me out like"—he snapped his fingers smartly—"this?"

"Yes."

"And he wants me to go? He has said so?"

She wanted no mistakes. "Not in so many words. But he says he'll back me up whatever I decide."

"So!" cried Zoltan, grasping at the faint gleam of hope. So it was she, not Mack, who was trying to destroy him. "Then I think I will speak to him myself before I start to pack."

"You mean you're refusing to go when I ask you?"

"I go when Mack asks me. I have rights."

"Rights! What rights?"

Zoltan thrust out his chin and chest, raising himself to his full height. His hands were trembling with rage; he clenched them into fists. Mack was his only hope. Could he count on him? Or would he sell out a brother for the fickle bitch who had once trapped him into marriage. Marriage was beyond him, but even he could see that this marriage was rotten and corrupt. Mack must know it too.

"I came to this house at invitation of your husband; I shall leave at his invitation also," he announced with dignity. His diction had grown increasingly formal, as if it were a secret source of strength. "Please tell him I have something to discuss. Tonight, if he is free . . . And now, if you don't mind to leave my room?"

He still dared to call it his room! Heather strained to contain her fury. "Tonight, then, when Mack gets home. We'll have one of our fabulous stimulating talks, Zoltan." She stood up, spilling the cat.

"I will ask Elaine to join us if possible, so Mack can hear from her own lips how preposterous is this mad idea of yours."

Heather glared. He would dare to bring his girlfriend into her house? "Okay, why don't you do that. And maybe I'll invite a second of my own."

For a moment familiar sparks flashed from the adversaries' gleaming eyes as they touched gloves before retreating to their separate corners.

"What time?"

"After I've put the kids to sleep. Say, nine?"

"Excellent. Now, if you will please excuse me . . ."

AS SOON AS SHE was gone Zoltan put on a sweater, then another. He felt cold, though his hands were sweaty and his mouth was dry. First you get kicked out for sleeping with someone's wife, then you get kicked out for not doing so. And just when the book was beginning to take shape, and he'd settled down enough to begin work. Exile was his lot, his realm, his Realm of Night.

He wanted to smash something. He tried pounding one fist into the other. Not enough. Then he picked up the thesaurus and slammed it down on the desk. Better. He did it again. He raked the fingers of both hands through his hair, pulling it back until his eyes were facing the ceiling. Finally, in a burst of rage he turned on the hot shower faucet full force and stripped off his clothes.

Water streamed over his body. They were closing in on him again. What did women want from him? They wanted to control him, bend him to their will, and when he resisted they became hysterical. Making scenes in public, screaming, crying, killing themselves, hounding him out of his home. When all one wanted was to be left in peace. Which was why he couldn't live with Elaine even if her place were twice as large and she could practice her cello elsewhere. It was as Maupassant wrote a century ago, in that story Orville and his friends knew almost by heart: "when a woman has picked out the lion she intends to bag, she stalks him with compliments, favors, little acts of kindness . . ." until she has eaten him alive—like "rats in a granary." Exactly!

He let the hot water cascade off his scalp, his shoulders. He remembered that hideous night he had been sleeping in Loretta's bed when suddenly a key turned in the outer lock, the front door opened, and there was her husband lumbering up the stairs. By that time the affair with Loretta had long since wound down, and they slept together only occasionally, when her husband was away. Why not? The betrayal had already occurred, they reasoned, and their sporadic coupling would make no difference. But her husband, a large, slow-moving man, seeing another man in his bed, could not possibly have understood. Without even removing his coat or boots he threw himself on top of Zoltan and began to pummel him methodically. Loretta, naked, tried to pull him off, whimpering and squealing; but Zoltan, who had once strenuously resisted arrest and once crossed two borders incognito, seeing the mammoth misunderstanding did not even try to defend himself. From that moment on, he swore off married women.

The hot water pelted his back and legs until steam saturated the air, filling his throat, his sinuses, his eyes and ears. It was almost unbearably hot, but he wanted it hotter still. He raised his arms high and turned toward the stream. As the hot liquid flowed down his chest, all but scalding his genitals, he felt his head begin to clear, his tense muscles relax.

Mack should be held responsible. Mack should give him severance pay and a relocation fee as penalty for being weak, for allowing Heather to rule him. The sort of man who found opportunity in the misfortunes of others, who cashed in on a market collapse, should be made to pay for the misery he caused. At the very least, he ought to use his real estate connections to find another place for him to live and subsidize his rent. He owed him that. Wasn't a husband responsible for his wife's debts? Tit for tat. Proudhon's dictum—Property is theft— certainly applied to Mack's, which was obtained not by labor but by cunning, even, as he himself acknowledged, by fraud. When the air was almost too thick to breathe, the water too hot to stand, he closed the hot faucet and opened the cold. Like a cold plunge after a sauna, like cold behavior following hot to demoralize your enemy, like the good-cop/bad-cop combo, an icy shower after a scalding one was a triumph of will and a powerful energizer. He needed every bit of will and energy he could command for the approaching trial.

When he was dry and dressed he picked up his cell and phoned Elaine.

22   BY EIGHT-THIRTY THE MOUNTAIN was covered with wet snow. If ever Mack was justified in being late, it would be tonight. No sooner did the wipers clear a swath through the windshield than fresh snow piled up again. The road was winding, with only one passable lane. The Porsche had a powerful engine, but in snow like this he needed four-wheel drive. He peered into the impenetrable dancing light thrown by his brights, then dimmed down to regular, then clicked up to the brights again.

This was one meeting he would not mind being late for. At work he prided himself on his shrewd handling of tricky meetings. But this one would be different. The flicker of hope he had for it was sparked by Zoltan's having called it at all, but Mack

could not imagine an explanation that would satisfy
him or pacify Heather. He hardly knew which disturbed him most: Zoltan's exploitation, Heather's
petulance, or his own hubris. For without doubt
he had set the whole thing going, had practically
begged to be taken in, taking Zoltan in.

Too bad he couldn't wave the Projects & Prospects list in Zoltan's face without giving himself
away, demand an accounting of the Balkan Freedom Fund, ask how many heady conversations
could pay for each insult. Stipend indeed! On the
contrary, he ought to charge Zoltan damages for so
grossly abusing them. Patronizing a patron, treating Heather like a housemaid, squandering his
gifts. Heather was right. Zoltan teach them how to
live? He could teach Zoltan a thing or two.

Even so, part of him was sorry to see the adventure end. It wasn't only that without Zoltan
around he would be less free to concentrate on the
L.A. deal, which now required his full attention, or
even that he would miss the exhilarating talk, the
satisfaction of serving art, Zoltan's gratitude. He
knew that after Zoltan left, the household would
probably revert to dull routine and petty resent-
ments, like the charred stubble left after a fire.
How quickly Heather's radiant face would shed its

glow. Their sensual knowledge of being powerfully seen would wither. In Heather's eyes Mack would revert to being an absent father, and in his own eyes an impostor, a hustler, a fraud.

Suddenly the headlights caught a pair of eyes, unmoving, in the center of the road: some small mammal frozen with fear. Instinctively Mack hit the brake. Too hard, too late: instead of stopping, the car, following the heartless law of inertia, continued straight ahead in a steady skid. "Move!" he shouted, frantically turning the wheel one way, then the other.

In an instant the car left the road and thudded into a tree. He should never have swerved to avoid those eyes; he should have hit the little bastard instead; he should have been driving the Subaru, he thought, as he cut the ignition and got out to survey the damage. The front bumper was hanging down, one fender was slightly dented, but miraculously, the headlights still shone. Lucky he'd been driving slowly. He wondered if the eyes had got away, and what kind of creature they belonged to: rabbit? woodchuck? squirrel? possum? He got the shovel out of the trunk and cleared a path behind the back wheels. Then he started up the car, put it into reverse, and after a few scary spins of the tires managed to back onto the road. He heard the front left tire scraping against the fender, but at least he was moving. Immensely relieved, he called Heather to tell her he'd be late and promised her to drive the rest of the way at a crawl.

WHEN MACK TELEPHONED WITH the news of his accident, a feeling of dread came over Heather. Often she had imagined just such an accident, usually fatal. In her dreams Mack would be at the wheel, sometimes in a car, sometimes a plane, sometimes nearby, sometimes far away—and not always while she was asleep in her bed, either. She couldn't help it, he was gone so much. She'd see him speeding along, oblivious of the danger, and then the scene would switch to someone somberly delivering the news, forever altering her life. If the dream had been colored blue, it would switch to orange; if silver, to red—the colors, she imagined, of dawn, of hope, of freedom.

Now, hearing about his accident, however slight, her mind's eye saw black. She could not picture what had happened, only what might have happened. He could have died there—and just when she had come to appreciate that he was on her side.

He could have died, leaving her and the children alone to fend for themselves.

Once when she was seven her father had crashed into a tree with her asleep in the passenger seat (the "death seat," he'd called it afterward). It had been a hot, sultry night and they'd been traveling home from a family reunion in a distant town. Maybe he'd fallen asleep at the wheel—she never knew. Wasn't her mother also in the car? If so, wouldn't she have been the one in the death seat, with Heather and her sister asleep in the back? All the details were fuzzy before the moment when she woke to find the push buttons of the car radio rolling in her lap, a great elm tree leaning on the windshield, and her father sobbing as he held her in his arms. Whenever she recalled that scene it was as vivid as if it had just happened; now it returned when she contemplated Mack's accident. Miraculously no one had been hurt—then and, if Mack was telling the truth, now as well.

She had always been impressed by the power of her dreams. (Hadn't they brought her Zoltan?— though reality had turned them sour.) Now she was appalled by it. When she hung up the phone she felt so weak she had to sit down, though there was still much to do in preparation for the meeting.

Even though the announcement of the accident had been delivered not by a stranger, as in her dreams, but by Mack himself, it was enough like her dreams that she couldn't stop thinking how close she had come to killing him.

23   HEATHER ARRANGED THE SEATING into two facing groups near the fire and flicked the indirect spots on the high beams, as if for a touring architectural jury. On the mantel sat a vibrant arrangement of seeds and leaves she and the children had collected before they went to bed. She put on a CD of minimalist flute music that Zoltan had once asked her not to play, then stared out the window at the huge snowflakes filling the sky, looking like white ashes as they danced around the path lights. The night was dramatic and portentous. She was pleased.

Barbara and Abe Rabin arrived first. Heather hugged each of them at the door. "Thanks so much for coming all the way up here in the snow," she said, taking their coats.

"Where do you want our boots?" asked Rabin, adding in a whisper, "Is he here?"

"Not yet."

"I don't know exactly what it is you want us to do," said Barbara, removing her hat and finger-combing her hair. She was wearing her contacts, high-heeled boots, and despite the cold a thin low-cut sweater.

"Nothing, really. I have no more idea of what he's planning than you do. I was flabbergasted when he called this meeting. I just need you for moral support."

Barbara gave Heather's hand a supportive squeeze. "Is he really refusing to leave?"

"So far."

Rabin harrumphed. "How can he? It's your house."

"Not to him it's not. He says it's Mack's house, though I told him it's in my name, which it happens to be. I also told him Mack agrees with me."

Rabin snorted, "Typical schnorrer maneuver."

Heather led them to the fireside. "Why don't you sit over here, okay? This will be our side. They can sit over there."

"They?" said Rabin, easing his large bearish frame into a chair.

"Yes. Zoltan is bringing his girlfriend. That's one of the reasons I need you here. So as not to be outnumbered."

Rabin was wrestling his sweater over his big head when the doorbell rang. Everyone braced up. Heather wondered if she ought to count it a victory that Zoltan had not let himself in with his key. She laid a finger against her lips for silence, then walked to the door.

"Come in, come in."

Zoltan averted his eyes, refusing to look at her. Adorned again in his signature black cape, with rubber galoshes, fur hat with earflaps down, and long striped scarf wound around his neck, he again appeared utterly strange to her, even after three months and a swanky new wardrobe. By contrast, the woman beside him looked quite ordinary, in a blue parka and high, black, thick-soled boots, if a bit too skinny and blond and made-up to please Heather, who watched her stamp her feet on the mat and drop her car keys into her pocket.

"Heather, may I present Elaine Glinka?" said Zoltan, laying on the accent. "Elaine, please meet Heather McKay."

"Glad to meet you," said Elaine. As they shook hands Heather noted with satisfaction that Elaine's mouth was asymmetrical, giving an impression of lurching slightly to the left, and her fingernails were deeply bitten.

"Me too." Heather held out her arms for their garments, but Zoltan waved her off. "Will keep them, thank you."

In the living room Zoltan stopped short at the sight of the Rabins. He looked around. "Where is Mack?"

"He had a slight accident on the road, but he should be along any minute," said Heather. "Barbara Rabin, Abe Rabin, Zoltan Barbu, and, uh, Elaine, uh . . ."

"Glinka."

"Glinka," repeated Heather. "Can I get you guys a drink? Or some coffee?"

"No thank you," said Zoltan. "We will wait in my room until Mack arrives." He executed a little bow. "Come, Elaine."

"Did you hear that?" whispered Barbara when they were out of earshot. "'My room,' he says."

"Quel nerve!" said Rabin, laughing and smacking his right fist against his left palm.

"Didn't I tell you?" said Heather, pouring out three glasses of Pinot Grigio, Rabin's with ice. Even without the wine she felt positively giddy.

"Very strange-looking fellow, I must say," said Rabin. "Like a visitation from a vampire movie."

"But I see the attraction," countered Barbara. "That amazing nose. And of course the accent."

"It's his voice, too, so deep," said Heather, "even if you don't always quite get what he's saying. That and the unnerving way he can cast a spell by fixing you with his eyes." She was embarrassed to be touting Zoltan's charms, when she knew they worked only on the susceptible, among whom she no longer counted herself. She suspected that to the Rabins his posturing must appear more bilious than brilliant, more pompous than profound. How typical of their odd ménage that no one else she knew had laid eyes on this man, on whom the family had so recklessly fixated for three remarkable months.

"What did you think of the girlfriend?" asked Barbara.

"Prrsh," said Rabin, blowing air through his lips dismissively.

"Not you, Abe. Heather."

Heather—who had several vivid thoughts about the girlfriend, though admittedly they had so far exchanged hardly more than gratuitous smiles—suddenly heard a thumping noise and frantically gestured for silence.

But the sound came from the back door, not Zoltan's room. Mack stamped his boots on the mat and entered, red-faced and puffing, trailing Tina behind him.

"COFFEE? A DRINK? SODA?" said Mack. "We have everything."

Zoltan and Elaine exchanged a secret look. "No, thank you," said Elaine.

"We're all set," said Barbara.

"Scotch, please," said Zoltan, "with soda and a twist, if you don't mind, thanks."

Mack fixed the drink and handed Zoltan a tall glass. "So," he said, pouring a finger of Scotch over ice for himself and sitting down beside Heather. "I understand you called this meeting, Z, so why don't you begin?"

Zoltan, who tightly clutched a messenger bag in his lap, cleared his throat, squared his shoulders, and blinked the lights on in his eyes, fixing Mack with the look that had once inspired confidence and hope. "Has your wife told you what she proposes?"

"Why don't you go ahead and tell me yourself," said Mack expansively. In the corner of his eye he saw Heather sitting cross-legged near the edge of her seat, the top leg moving rapidly up and down from the knee, her arms folded over her fuzzy white sweater, her face flushed and defiant. This bickering was like children's, like family, with Mack the Solomonic judge and the Rabins the requisite witnesses. He leaned back and spread his arms along the back of the sofa.

"One day she loves me and the next day she proposes me to leave," Zoltan began, testing.

Slowly stroking Tina, who was curled up in her lap, Heather smiled impassively. She knew who was luxury in Mack's life, who necessity.

Mack nodded.

"And you go along with her?"

"Heather's the one who's home with you, so it's her call."

"Why? Is big house. I try not to bother her. In fact, Heather sees me only when for her own reasons she chooses." He glowered. "Did she tell you her reasons?"

Mack shrugged. "Heather's reasons are her business," he said, with a vague wave of the hand.

"I think you will find they are your business too."

Heather glowered back. "Mack knows my reasons. Right, Mack?" If Zoltan dared to spell out the details, she would simply dispute them. Her word against his. No contest—especially since nothing had actually happened.

Mack patted Heather's knee.

Seeing the smug gesture, Zoltan was tempted to tell Mack all about his lovely little wife. But with Elaine there to witness, he chose to take the moral high road rather than sink to Heather's level. If there was any chance of salvaging his position in the house it would be by appealing to Mack's sense of justice. Or his mercy. He wasn't evil, like her, only weak. A weak wretch. (Weak wretch: he liked the sound of it; he must remember to write it down.)

"You realize, of course, I have no money. And if I leave here I have no place to go. I can't go back to L.A., my apartment is long ago gone to landlord's relative. And until I sell my book I can't pay rent. As you well knew when you invited me here to live and sent me my airline ticket."

"Pooh. You could always sign a contract and get some money," said Mack. "You have a name to sell. Or apply for a stipend from that Balkan Freedom Fund of yours, get them to use my donation."

Zoltan crossed his arms and raised his nose haughtily. "You think such money sits wasting in some drawer or bank? It is already spent for good purpose."

"Oh, really? For what, I'd like to know. Would you happen to have the records?"

"You have so many friends, Zoltan," interrupted Heather. "Some of them must be dying to put you up. What about Elaine here? Why don't you move in with her?"

Zoltan looked triumphant. Heather had sprung the trap. With his eyes he signaled to Elaine.

"Excuse me. He can't possibly move in with me," said Elaine.

"Why not? He's there most nights anyway," said Heather, focusing on the oddly crooked mouth.

"For one thing," said Zoltan, "she has not invited me."

"My place is much too small for two. It's just a studio, really, and it's also where I practice."

"Not too tiny for two at night, though, is it?"

Elaine rolled her eyes at Zoltan, as if Heather's outrageous behavior confirmed everything he had said about her, while Mack could barely suppress a laugh over Heather's chutzpah. He had to admit his wife was one cool brazen bitch.

"You're welcome to come and see it, if you don't believe me," offered Elaine.

"Really, this is preposterous," exploded Zoltan. He turned to Elaine and clasped her hands. "You don't have to do this. You don't have to defend your choice to live alone."

"What about Rebecca Shaffer, then?" said Heather. "She has a huge loft. Right in the middle of Soho, very convenient."

"That is the problem," said Zoltan, finally looking at Heather. "It is also only one room, though very big one. But this is moot. No one invites me there."

"She would in a minute if she knew you were interested."

"Maybe, maybe not. It is also her husband's place. In any case," he continued, "I could not work there, in same house with another writer. She would eat me up alive."

"Well, you don't seem to be able to work here either," mumbled Mack.

Heather was too proud to point out that in this house, too, another writer lived, since Zoltan had never acknowledged it.

"Fact is, my man," said Zoltan, "you are the only person who invites me to stay. No one else has offered."

"Well, now we're withdrawing our offer," said Heather.

"Does she speak for you?" Zoltan asked Mack.

"I'm speaking for myself," said Heather.

"Why, may I ask?"

"Why what?"

"Why are you withdrawing invitation?"

"I told you why this morning."

"And did you tell also your husband?"

"Yes, more or less."

"More or less." He spat it out with his familiar sneer. "Will you tell him now please exactly what you told me this morning, exactly why you ask me to leave? Would you repeat in front of your husband?"

"Sure."

Barbara Rabin sat entranced at the edge of her seat trying to follow the words slamming back and forth like Ping-Pong balls, while her husband jiggled the cubes in his glass with an expression of amused distaste.

"I'm asking you to leave," said Heather, determination in her raised chin, "because in your three months with us in this house you haven't come through for me."

"And how is that, please? What do I withhold?"

"Everything."

"Meaning?"

"Didn't you come here promising to teach us something important, the secret of happiness or something like that? But you can't teach us anything when you're gone all night and you sleep all day. Why should we keep you here when there's nothing in it for us anymore? Why? What claim do you have on us? That's what I'd like to know."

Zoltan shook his head and sent a long eloquent look to Elaine. Then he took a sip of Scotch and taunted Heather with "Pardon me, I fail to see how my sleeping arrangements concern you."

"After you move out they won't. Which is why I want you to leave."

Zoltan turned to Mack with an exasperated shrug. "Can't you do something about this, my good man? You invited me here, not she. You have not said for me to go. It means you are unconvinced. At least ambivalent."

It was this Mack would miss—how easily Zoltan saw through him. Now, with Zoltan backed into a corner, Mack couldn't help feeling sorry for the guy. Talk about ambivalence! Even if he did pocket the donation, which wasn't all that much, the fellow had to live somehow. Whatever he did or didn't do, he was still the author of "one of the landmark works of the twentieth century," according to the *New Republic*, still a scintillating presence, and admired for that prison time—if it was true. And if not, one had to admire a guy who could put it over on the world.

All the same, it was Mack's duty to back up Heather. "I'm afraid you're wrong there, Z. I happen to agree with her."

"I see. You fall back on marriage and let your wife decide for you. You give up responsibility. I thought you were more man than that. I see I am wrong."

"Responsibility?" Heather blurted out. "You want to talk responsibility?"

"Certainly. Who is responsible should take consequences. Mack cannot leave me stranded, he must make good on his promise. If not, he is a weak wretch, cowardly fool like Samson—"

"Come, now," interrupted Mack. "There's no point getting personal. Fact is I promised you a place to write, but you aren't writing, are you?"

"Yes I am."

"Oh? Then where's the book?"

"Book is not finished. But I have many pages of notes and drafts. Probably too many. That is my problem. Writing is harder than you imagine."

While Mack sipped his drink and the Rabins sat in their front-row seats in riveted silence watching the drama unfold, the room's only sound was the crackle of logs reducing to embers.

"Anyway," said Mack, "it's really not a question

of who's responsible. Let's just say we all gave it a
decent trial, and it's nobody's fault if things aren't
working out anymore, that's all."

"Things not working out. What you mean is,
certain people do not allow things to work out.
Matter of fact," said Zoltan, "it is very personal.
Matter of fact, your wife wants me to go because
you are not enough man for her. Not man enough
to control her."

"Slow down, Z," said Mack. "You're starting to
get out of line here."

Heather's heart was thumping. Zoltan was
coming dangerously close to the edge. She saw the
vein pulsing in his neck, as it always did when he
was seriously worked up. Still, whatever he said, it
was her house, and she had the final say. Let him
insult Mack and threaten her all he liked, nothing
would change her mind. If he shut up right now,
she'd give him as much time as he needed; if he
stepped one more inch over the line, she'd kick
him out tonight.

As moments passed in portentous silence, the
kind Zoltan could orchestrate to perfection, Abe
Rabin wondered if he as resident psychiatrist
shouldn't be doing something to defuse the tension. Barbara and Elaine watched Zoltan and

Heather, arms crossed over their chests, glaring fe-
rociously at each other. Mack leaned his head back
waiting to see which one would back down first.

Zoltan suddenly stood up, raised his glass high,
and with flaming eyes vaulted across the hearth toward Heather.

Mack sprang to his feet. "Whoa!" he cried, as
Rabin leaped in front of Heather and grabbed
Zoltan's arm. The two stood clinched for a moment, pumping arms, like fake TV wrestlers, until
Zoltan's Scotch began to spill on the rug and Rabin
stepped back. In that instant Zoltan hurled his
glass into the flames, where it shattered, the rem-
nants of liquid fizzling into steam.

Elaine cowered. Mack downed his drink. Barbara rushed to embrace Heather. But Heather,
having seen this shattered-glass melodrama one
too many times, knew that the curtain had been
pulled aside to reveal the wizard's sham. Out of
danger, she laughed with relief.

"Come, then," said Zoltan softly to Elaine, re-
gaining enough dignity to offer her his hand. Anything more he might say would be anticlimactic.
He pulled her to her feet, all courtesy and calm.
"Come. We will get our coats and I will take you
home."

As they left the room Rabin whispered to Barbara, "What he means is, is she'll take him home."

"I APOLOGIZE TO YOU, my dear, for subjecting you to this ugliness," said Zoltan, as he and Elaine loaded his bags into the trunk of her car.

"Forget it."

Snow quickly powdered their hats and boots. When they were done, she cleared off the windshield while he returned to the house, where his hosts and their guests sat gossiping.

Wordlessly he walked up to Mack, who was just then poking the fire. Slivers of broken glass sparkled on the hearth. Suddenly alert, Mack turned around, clutching the poker in both hands. Zoltan stood before him wearing a twisted, superior smile. With an exaggerated flourish he handed Mack the house keys, then bowed deeply, Karamazov style, his long forelock sweeping the floor and his boots leaving little puddles on the hearth. The flames shot up; except for the fire, the room was again silent. Then without so much as a glance at Heather or the Rabins, Zoltan raised himself to his full height, elevated his nose, turned, and left. Silence reigned until the outer door slammed closed. Still no one spoke as the car motor started, died, started again, warmed up, and finally receded as the car drove away. Then a collective sigh relieved the tension, and Mack traded the poker for the hearth broom and began sweeping up glass.

"Here, let me do that," said Barbara, taking the broom from Mack while he got the dustpan. When all the broken glass had been swept up Mack carried the dustpan to the kitchen.

"So what did you think of him?" asked Heather.

"A narcissistic, self-dramatizing sociopath. I can't imagine what you see in him, Heather," said Rabin.

"Saw," corrected Heather.

"No, Abe," said Barbara, "he's much too large a personality to just write off like that. He may be a sociopath, but sociopaths can be very attractive. I can see what they saw in him, even in that getup. You've got to admit you've never met anyone like him. He's a throwback to some other age. Further back than a hippie . . . maybe some nineteenth-century bohemian type, part ascetic, part dandy, part I don't know what. Someone out of *La Bohème* or *The Count of Monte Cristo*. The goatee, that capey thing, tossing a glass into the fire!"

"Dracula maybe?" drawled Rabin. "Fin de siècle but of the wrong siècle."

"Not that he wouldn't be totally impossible to live with," Barbara conceded with a nod to Heather, "I can see that he's somewhat unhinged. But still, most charlatans are charismatic—that's how come they can pull it off. I half expected him to challenge Mack to a duel, or pull a rapier out from under his cloak."

"Or a horsewhip," said Heather.

"Or sink his fangs into Heather," said Rabin.

"If Heather didn't sink her fangs into him first," said Mack, who had just returned from the kitchen carrying a tray with a bottle of vintage port and four fresh glasses. He winked affectionately at Heather.

"Barbara's got the charlatan part right," said Rabin, "but I'd say he's more the vitamin salesman type of charlatan."

"You've got it," said Mack, putting his arm around his wife. "A vitamin salesman! Offering the secret elixir of life."

"And a ladies' man," added Barbara.

"A scoundrel and a cad," said Rabin.

Heather said wistfully, "All of the above."

"I SHOULD WARN YOU," said Mack when the Rabins were ready to leave, "there may be a dead animal about five miles down the road. I think I hit something on my way home tonight. I skidded trying to avoid it and ran into a tree. Smashed a fender. Lucky I got back here in one piece."

"Which car were you driving?" asked Rabin.

"Unfortunately, the Porsche."

"What kind of animal was it? I'll keep an eye out."

"Can't really say. All I know is I caught the eyes in my headlights, swerved to avoid killing it, and went into a skid. Poor bastard probably didn't know what hit him."

"Just like Zoltan," quipped Barbara, grinning.

Mack gave her a look and continued, "*If* I hit him. I don't remember a thud, and there was no body I could see, so there's a chance I only grazed him and he got away. Which might be even worse for the poor bastard. I feel really bad about it."

Heather, who loved animals, was willing to sacrifice this one in exchange for Mack. "Not your fault, Mack. It was an accident," she said, reaching a hand out to comfort him.

"That's pretty generous coming from you, babe," said Mack, "since you always say you don't believe in accidents."

24   EARLY THE NEXT MORNING, while Heather was carrying an armful of files up-stairs to her reclaimed study, she noticed that the table where the de Kooning belonged was naked, with a faint ring of dust around the spot where the sculpture usually sat. She looked on the floor, then around the hall. Nothing. It must have been stolen.

Her heart started to pound. She knew she ought to report the theft to Mack immediately but was reluctant because she knew he'd suspect Carmela. He'd be wrong: Carmela would never have left a dust ring. That meant it had to be Zoltan. He must have slipped it under his cloak on the way out, to make fools of them and have the last laugh.

If he expected her to sit by and let him, he was wrong. Such ingratitude! Feeling violated and duped, she had half a mind to call 911 and send the police straight down to Elaine's, where they could arrest him for grand larceny. Then nothing could save him from prison or deportation except her mercy. Let him beg her for it. Only if he immediately returned the sculpture would she even consider withholding charges.

She ran to the great room to check on the rest of the art: the Hockney, the Motherwell, the Wesley, the Salle—each piece irreplaceable, however well insured. They were all there on the walls where they belonged, encircling the room, like gems on a necklace—

Her jewelry! She suddenly pictured it laid out in its drawer, so vulnerable and precious and portable. She ran downstairs.

The drawer was still locked, the key tucked into a bra among her lingerie, where it belonged. All the same, she did a quick inventory of her favorite pieces. Nothing was obviously missing, though she knew it might be weeks, perhaps months, before she could be sure that he hadn't swiped something she treasured to present to some other woman.

Now she needed to survey the damage. She checked the cars in the garage, the electronics in the den, the silver in the pantry. Nothing was noticeably out of order, but until they checked the insurance inventory she couldn't know for sure what else he might have taken or which valuable pieces might be missing.

When there was nothing else to check on, she phoned Mack in Chicago to break the news.

Although Mack was outraged, with hindsight he was not surprised. Zoltan's expression when he left the house after that floor-sweeping final bow had been too sardonic; Mack should have suspected he had something up his sleeve. When it came to power plays, Mack was used to men's hardball.

After he got control of his outrage, he felt something approaching elation. Not that he wasn't concerned for his de Kooning (though it was fully insured, and there were living artists he'd as soon collect instead). But now he no longer had any doubt that between the two of them, Mack and Zoltan, Zoltan was the greater fraud. Mack may have lost an artwork, but he had won the game. This theft was the proof—though no doubt Zoltan held an opposite opinion.

"We were pussycats, Heather. We should have known when he took my diamond cufflinks that sooner or later he'd pull off some stunt like this."

"And the laptop is gone too."

"He took your laptop? He can't even use it very well."

"Not because I didn't try to teach him."

"This proves what he's been after all along, in case you had any lingering doubts. Have you notified the police?"

"Not yet."

"That's good. Because I sure wouldn't want to make him a martyr at our expense."

"How could he be the martyr?!"

"Think about it. Well-known writer versus real estate developer, that's how it would play. You know as well as I do that developers don't rouse much sympathy. Imagine the headlines: DISTINGUISHED ÉMIGRÉ AUTHOR SENTENCED TO PRISON IN DISPUTE WITH DEVELOPER. And the Letters to the Editor: Mogul vs. Hero. Plus he's got all those fancy literary friends to form a defense committee and start a campaign against me on the Internet. I sure don't need the negative publicity—especially now, in this economy, and when I've applied for a big tax abatement in L.A. In any PR contest, I'm afraid we'd lose. We'd be better off just to collect the insurance and move on."

"Don't we have to make a police report before we can file an insurance claim?"

"We'll report it without mentioning Zoltan. We'll think of some other scenario, maybe a burglary—"

"But a burglar would have grabbed other things besides one small bronze sculpture."

"And the laptop. Anyway, babe, at this point we have no idea what else he may have taken."

"I checked my jewelry. I don't think anything's missing there. I didn't check yours, though. Remember, Mack, he did return your cufflinks when I asked him to. Maybe he'll return this too."

"First we've got to find him. I'll come home as soon as I can. I'll call you. Meanwhile, if he's not at Elaine's, you can start calling around to his friends, see if you can locate him. It's very important that we maintain control of the situation."

IT WAS AFTER MIDNIGHT when Mack pulled the snow-covered Subaru into the garage. Uncharacteristically, Heather was there at the door waiting to fall into his arms. "Oh, Mack!" she cried, clinging to him. "I feel so awful! So violated!"

For a while, right there in the utility room, under the watchful eyes of newts, they hugged each other and kissed, closing ranks. As they walked downstairs to their bed it was understood that, despite the hour, they would make love.

Surprisingly intense, their sex that night embodied a new closeness in the face of adversity. Which perhaps was why, when they were finished, neither of them could fall asleep, though the clock read after two.

"Did you find out where he is? Does anyone know?" asked Mack.

"Not Elaine or the Shaffers—unless they're lying. Do you think they'd cover for him? Be accessories to his crime? Accessories after the fact, as it's called on *Law and Order*."

"I doubt he'd tell anybody about the theft. To get his friends to hide him he'd only have to concoct some horror story about us."

"Or he could say we gave him the sculpture as a gift."

"Like a rapist who claims his victim asked for it," said Mack.

"If we knew he was just acting impulsively to get back at us for kicking him out, it wouldn't feel so bad," said Heather. "It might even be sort of funny—you know: all's fair in love and war? It would certainly make a funny story. But if he's viewed us as marks all along and has just been waiting for the right moment to make fools of us—"

Mack was of the opinion that if anyone was made a fool of, it was Zoltan, not them. First for wasting this once-in-a-lifetime opportunity, and then for indulging in a foolish crime, for which he was bound to be caught. A moment of indulgence for a lifetime of regret. Stupid.

"I'll check some pawnshops. The piece will turn up if he tries to dump it. Hot art is very hard to sell because there's a paper trail. Wherever it is," said Mack, "once we bring in the insurance company it's just a matter of time till they catch him and prosecute. Those lawyers don't fuss around. Which is why I want to find him first. I wonder if he realizes the danger he's in."

"I should have taken back my laptop as soon as I told him to leave," said Heather. "I should have made a point of it, like I did with the cufflinks, let him know it mattered. Since I didn't, he might have figured we wouldn't miss the de Kooning either."

"Nonsense. Get it through your head, babe: this is not your fault. He knew what he was doing. He may be hoping we won't report it, but he's probably scared to death. Or ought to be. Poor Zoltan."

"Poor Zoltan? Are you kidding?" Heather was amazed that after everything that had happened, Mack could still honor that primal bond. "We're the victims here, Mack, not him. Or have you forgotten?"

"I doubt if he sees it that way."

"So what? How do you see it?"

Content that he had won his contest with Zoltan, Mack felt he could afford to be magnanimous. But Heather, who had lost hers, couldn't. Preferring not to rile her further, he answered, "All I want now is to get back the de Kooning with the least publicity."

"I'll bet he's laughing at us this very minute, knowing we won't have the nerve to press charges."

"If it comes to that, which I hope it doesn't, we shall see," said Mack.

"Being ripped off always feels like a brutal violation, even when a stranger does it, like when my purse was snatched in Rome by that guy whizzing by on a Vespa? But when it's someone you thought was your friend, then it's a terrible assault. The worst part is the betrayal. That's what really hurts. You just can't believe that a friend, someone you were close to, someone you may even have loved, would do that to you." She felt her throat closing down again. No tears!

"He probably feels the same way about us."

"How do you mean?"

"You know. Betrayed."

"He should feel disgraced, not betrayed," said Heather indignantly.

"Did I tell you what he said to me when I took him shopping for clothes? He was being fitted by the tailor when he turned to me and quoted Andrew Carnegie. 'The man who dies rich dies disgraced.'"

Heather laughed. "Imagine! Andrew Carnegie! He was probably just trying to save you from disgrace, Mack, by making you a little less rich. Isn't that what he promised? To save you?"

Mack was glad to see Heather lighten up. He thought he might be able to sleep now. Each one switched off a light and snuggled down in the dark. But Heather kept on smiling. "You want to know what he said to me?"

"What?"

"To me he quoted Proudhon. He said, 'Property is theft.'"

"Oh! That explains everything," said Mack.

When they were done laughing, Mack again took her in his arms. "I guess I should apologize for bringing him here, babe. I'm sorry for what he put you through. But it's almost over. Now we're going to find him and get the piece back and move on. I promise."

"No, don't be sorry. I'm not. Actually I'm glad. I wouldn't have missed it for anything."

"You know something? Me too," said Mack, kissing her one last time, content that his scheme had succeeded after all.

ZOLTAN CHECKED HIS PASSPORT and patted his wallet. He was drinking a final Scotch on the rocks in the business lounge as he waited for his plane to be called. His ticket was in coach but, having seriously considered traveling first class, he felt he deserved the lounge's amenities. In the end, despite carrying a wad of dollars in his pocket and having donned his fashionable clothes, prudence had made him opt for coach.

It burned him that he'd got only a fraction of what the de Kooning was worth, but he'd been in no position to shop around, much less to be greedy. Every minute counted. Sufficient that there was plenty of money to get him to Paris before Heather turned him in and enough left over to live on—even in style—till he decided what to do next. They owed him at least that. If he had to flee, it couldn't have happened at a more opportune time. News from his country was breaking fast. If the rumored uprisings succeeded, and the dictator's party didn't stage a comeback, there was a good chance he could return home a hero. The prospect so tickled him that he laughed out loud. Hadn't the playwright Havel led the Velvet Revolution and become president of the Czech Republic? Not that Zoltan had political ambitions, but if Malraux could be a minister of culture, conceivably so could he. A good professorship would perhaps be more suitable, but given the volatile atmosphere, anything was possible.

Meanwhile, his years in Hollywood and Sontag's extravagant praise would give him all the clout he needed for reentry into Paris. Perhaps he would treat himself to a good hotel from which to renew his contacts. And sport again his Parisian ascot.

Hearing his flight announced, he leaped up, crushed out his cigarette, and drained his glass. He hoisted his backpack to one shoulder, his laptop to the other, and proceeded to the gate. His seat was near the front of the plane and they were loading from the rear. Good. He was finished with America—in his mind he was already gone.

As he waited for his row to be called, he patted his wallet again. He regretted that he had been unable to say good-bye to the people who had been kind to him, but secrecy and speed precluded all contact. He hoped that at least the Shaffers would understand. He had only one unshakable regret:

that he hadn't fucked out the brains of that crazy Heather McKay. A prime opportunity squandered; stupidly wasted virtue. She asked for it and Mack deserved it. But then, he mused, he would have returned her to Mack in better condition than he found her, which meant that both of them would have got what they wanted from him after all, while he got nothing in return. The de Kooning didn't count, being the least they owed him for his pains, whether he'd fucked her or he hadn't. Better that he had not, he consoled himself—without, however, altering his regret.

His row was called. Heart booming, he shuffled along the line. It was strictly out of habit that he zapped the stewardess with piercing eyes and the faintest hint of a courtly bow as he showed his passport, handed her his ticket, and walked on up the ramp.

25 SEARCH AS THEY TRIED, they couldn't find Zoltan, not even with the help of a private detective close to Interpol. After a brief interlude in Paris, he evidently vanished. How a man of such distinctive looks could disappear was a mystery no one ever solved, not even when the de Kooning turned up at a specialty fence in Brooklyn, long after Mack had used the insurance check to buy a Jeff Koons that he'd had his eye on. Nothing lost: Mack simply returned the money to the insurance company and kept both pieces for his collection.

Zoltan, however, did not turn up. If his friends knew where he was they weren't telling.

In the months following his disappearance, entrancing rumors about him occasionally surfaced on the Internet and drifted back to the McKays: that he'd disappeared underground, though with that nose it would have been difficult; that he had fled to Chechnya on false papers provided by the CIA; that he had slipped back into his native country to help foment a revolt; that he had suffered a massive heart attack; that he had written another stunning book under a nom de plume. But none of the rumors was ever confirmed, and after a while they stopped.

Nevertheless, at the house on the mountain, Zoltan's legacy remained alive. Soon after his departure, with the children enrolled in school all day, Heather was back in the room he had occupied, working furiously on her own stories, Tina sleeping at her feet. Above her desk to inspire her hung a photo of Zoltan, one Mack had taken shortly after he'd joined their ménage. There he was, matted on dark red velvet, looking animatedly out of an antique walnut frame, black lock falling forward, lips pursed in that characteristic smirk, hawk nose tilted, arms folded across his chest—provocative, austere, alluring, eyes gleaming fiercely. Not unlike the leering picture of Gurdjieff in the Mansfield biography, she sometimes thought, or the famous portrait of Rasputin with the mesmerizing eyes.

Every time she sat down to work Heather exulted in the ironic triumph that Zoltan had imparted the promised secret after all. His negative example and the paltry contents of his trash had exploded the mystique of the writer's life that had once both daunted and seduced her, freeing her to settle down to work (as he, despite his fame, had not managed to do, she reflected snarkily). The very discipline and determination that had eluded him now fortified her. No matter that he was a thief, his vaunted knowledge a sham, or that a month after his departure neither Chloe nor Jamie had a single memory of the man pictured in the photo over Heather's desk, as if he had not existed. When opportunity knocks, you seize it, even if it means sucking blood from a vampire. Gurdjieff, too, she remembered—and Rasputin, for that matter—was widely regarded as a charlatan, his powers as fugitive as mist, as subtle as air, though that did not prevent Katherine Mansfield, Margaret Anderson, and other literary notables from giving absolute devotion to their master in exchange for some elusive but precious value. Whenever her writing bogged down, she was able to give it a jump start by summoning Zoltan's astonished face on the day, fast approaching, when he would hold in his hands her book of stories, dedicated to him. (How they would reach him she hadn't yet figured out.) Ah, then wouldn't he regret having dismissed her work and turned her down!

Mack found a different consolation. The insult of Zoltan's bilking his own benefactors enabled Mack to write him off as a bad investment—a lesson he'd early mastered at the Business School. The next time he felt charitable toward the arts, he decided, he'd fund a fellowship or endow a prize. Now that his biggest gamble, the L.A. deal, had succeeded, and his tax abatement had been granted in full, he was able to laugh off the insult, like Liberace on the way to the bank. Already, long before completion, the project was almost fully rented, with a small apartment reserved for himself and Vicky D., his new girlfriend (or, as Zoltan would say, "mistress"), who happened to look remarkably like Maja Stern. Sometimes, sitting opposite Vicky at La Mer, peering down at her plump Hollywood breasts, Mack imagined she was Maja reincarnated. But the resemblance ended with the physical, for she wanted much more of him than to be a mere dinner companion. With one successful boutique and plans to expand (with a little venture capital from him), she was not the type to threaten scandal or suicide; and though, as he sometimes thought, she might harbor a secret wish to capture him, she knew better than to bug him as Maja had bugged Zoltan or to even think of asking him to leave his wife.

ABOUT THE AUTHOR

ALIX KATES SHULMAN is the author of the feminist classic *Memoirs of an Ex-Prom Queen* and three other novels; three memoirs, including the award-winning *Drinking the Rain*; two books on the anarchist Emma Goldman; and *A Marriage Agreement and Other Essays*. Her work has been translated into twelve languages, her essays have appeared in the *New York Times*, *Salon*, *The Nation*, and *The Guardian*. She lives in New York City. www.alixkshulman.com